The Moon
is
Blue

Martyn Hesford

ISBN: 9798478318680

PublishNation

For Keith Sumner

someone said

> "we read other people's stories
> so we can understand our own"

This is my story...

CHAPTER 1

Dream

The night before my 16th birthday,
something strange
happened.

A dream,
and my dream
went like this…

I was lying in bed, then all of a sudden, I was floating out of the window, I was floating over fields of flowers. The flowers were different colours, they were glowing like a thousand electric lightbulbs. Ever so bright and colourful, like the coloured lights on a Christmas tree. They smelt of my favourite sweets, and I thought to myself, what a way to travel! It beats riding on a bus.

And when I thought of a bus ride, I thought of her, sat next to me, like the day she gave me the gift of the blue rose. And when I thought of her, there she was, lying next to me.

Both floating over the fields of electric lightbulb flowers.

Together.
Holding hands.

And when I looked down, one of the flowers sparkled more than the others. Its light was so bright. I knew the light meant something, but I wasn't sure what. Until suddenly the light shone even brighter, a flame,
and
it burst
into

blue.

CHAPTER 2

Magic

The first time she appeared, the lady in blue was sat up in the branches of a tree. Me and George were playing a game in the park.

"Look at her," I said.

"Who?"

"That lady sat up in a tree."

"Oh yes," said George, "what's she doing?"

"Perhaps she's bird-watching?"

"No she's not," said George, "she's watching us."

"Am I, dear?" said the lady.

Her voice was mysterious.
Her words floated down
to us
like snowflakes.

Magic.

CHAPTER 3

Hovering

The second time she appeared, the lady in blue was hovering over the chip shop.

"...She's back," I said.

George looked up into the air.

"Oh yes," he said, "and she's staring again. Nosey thing."

George is my best friend. He lives next door. My name's Florence, I've always been called Flo. I'm nine years old and George is nine and three quarters. Me and George go to the same school, and we both go to the same chip shop for our tea. Mum goes to the bingo a lot, and Dad doesn't cook. George's dad is never at home. He goes to the pub most days and stays till late. George hasn't got a mum, she died of something serious in her lungs a few months back. They found a lump. The chip shop is around the corner, next to the gas works. It's called "Mary's Plaice". We live in Manchester.

"That's a good trick she's doing," said George, "hovering."

"Perhaps she's a magician's assistant," I said.

"No," said George, "magician's assistants usually wear sequinned bras with sparkly shoes."

"That's true," I said. "I saw one on the telly. She had a poodle and three white rabbits."

The lady in blue didn't have any of these things. She didn't even wear shoes.

CHAPTER 4

Mystery

"Who is she? I wonder?"

The two of us were standing in my kitchen eating biscuits.

"Perhaps she's from a circus," I said.

"Yes," said George. "They have a circus every Easter in the park. I went there when Mum was alive. It was good."

"She could be a tight rope walker?" I said.

"No," said George, "I don't think so, because she wasn't wearing any tights, we could see her bare feet. She didn't even do the splits. She just floated."

"Perhaps she's some kind of flying acrobat?" I said.

"No," said George. "Wearing that long blue, floaty dress, if she tried to do a somersault, she'd get herself tangled up, wouldn't she?"

"That's true." I said.

It was a mystery.

CHAPTER 5

Unbelievers

"You're a liar," said Julie.

"I'm not," I said.

"You're making things up."

"I'm not making anything up."

"A lady in blue? Hovering over the chip shop? Get a life. What do you think I am?"

I wanted to say "stupid" but I thought, no, better not. Don't get Julie annoyed (she'd only start spitting at me again). I'd met Julie walking into school. I wish I hadn't said anything about the lady in blue. George warned me to keep it our secret. He said nobody would believe us. He said it was our story. Nobody else's. I suppose I was showing off, telling Julie about it. Me and her were always in competition. She lived in a big house on the new development, and I lived in a pokey old house on the 'no go' estate. Our estate was waiting to be knocked down. It was full of tyres, bicycle frames, bits of cars, burnt out motor bikes, and smells. Julie seemed to have everything and I seemed to have nothing. I was the girl that wore cheap National Health glasses. Julie was the girl who wore golden trainers. She also had an earring through her nose. There was even a rumour she'd got a tattoo on her bum, saying "Princess". I hadn't seen it, but a boy in school said he'd seen it twice during swimming. Julie had shown it off for a fiver. She wasn't shy. That was the rumour, anyway.

"What are you two girls arguing about?" said Miss Tickle (our teacher).

"Flo Hargreaves claims she saw a woman flying over the chip shop, Miss."

"Really? Was the woman drunk?"

I could tell Miss Tickle didn't believe me. Miss Tickle was making fun. I tried not to let this bother me.

"The woman was dressed in blue and wore no shoes," I said. "Her hair was long and her face was lovely."

"You're a liar," said Julie. "It's just a pathetic, made up story, to brighten your sad life."

"Yes it is," said Miss Tickle.

Julie smiled. She liked Miss Tickle. They were mates. Julie's mum and Miss Tickle shared the same personal fitness instructor, and always went jogging together.

"I'm not making anything up," I said. "The lady in blue exists. Honest."

"Would you please carry my new designer handbag, Julie," said Miss Tickle.

"And you, Flo Hargreaves, get into that classroom and tidy up my drawers."

Julie and Miss Tickle walked through the school playground together, arm in arm. I stood watching and blew my nose. I could tell they were talking about me, the way they both smirked.

Unbelievers.

CHAPTER 6

Flew

At 7 o'clock that night, it happened again.

"I bet you didn't expect to see me here?" said the lady in blue, waving (from inside the telly!). I heard a muffled cry through the wall. It was George, next door.

"Can George see you, too?" I asked, amazed.

"Yes," said the lady in blue. "George can see me next door inside his own telly, just like you."

"Who are you talking to?" asked Mum, bewildered.

I ignored her. Mum got up and violently hit the telly.

"What you doing, Mum?"

"What does it look like I'm doing? I'm trying to make the telly work. The screen's gone fuzzy. There's no picture."

"Hit it harder, Marlene," said Dad, eating a cake, and dribbling cream down his chin. "Give it a good kick."

Mum hit the telly again (only harder) and gave it a good kick. I realised that Mum and Dad couldn't see the lady in blue. All they could see was a fuzzy TV screen.

"Don't hide away behind the sofa, George," said the lady in blue, "I won't harm you."

I thought of George hiding behind his sofa next door and began to smile. He was scared.

"He thinks you're a ghost, your ladyship," I said.

"Does he, indeed?"

"Yes. He thinks you've come to haunt us. Ha ha."

"Who are you talking to?" asked Dad.

I ignored him.

"You're not a ghost, are you?" I said.

"Of course not, silly. I'm your... friend."

Oh, I was pleased the lady in blue said this. It made me feel good.

But then, something strange and very peculiar happened...

around the lady in blue's head
a crown of stars appeared,
swirling
(like exploding fireworks).

The swirling stars
got brighter and brighter.

Then...
the lady in blue
flew
out of the telly
and floated
around
the room.

CHAPTER 7

Stars

There were lots of little stars bursting all around the lady in blue's body. It was frightening and beautiful at the same time. She was smiling and I heard singing, somewhere, like a choir at a wedding when the bride comes in. The lady in blue kept on floating and the choir kept on singing, "Ahhhhhhhhhhhhh." And just when I thought she might explode into one big huge massive rainbow, the lady in blue... just... disappeared and the choir went quiet and the weather man appeared on the telly.

"It's raining in Manchester." he said. "Don't forget your wellies."

"Thank goodness for that," said Mum. "Normal service resumed."

I sat there, staring. The colours (blue, red and white, whirling in my head).

"What's up with our Flo?" said Mum.

I said nothing. I didn't know what happened. I hadn't a clue. I felt... strange.

"She looks a bit peeky," said Dad.

"Are you sickening for something, pet?" asked Mum.

"She looks like she's seen a ghost," said Dad.

"She's not a ghost," I said

Who's not a ghost?" asked Mum

"The lady in blue," I said. "She's... my friend."

CHAPTER 8

Wonky

"When did you first start seeing ghosts?" asked Doctor Cronk.

"Flo started seeing ghosts last night, Doctor," said Mum.

"I see," said Doctor Cronk, gravely.

"And what did this vision say to you, Florence?"

"The lady in blue says she's my friend."

"Really?" said Doctor Cronk. "How peculiar."

I could tell he didn't believe me.

"What do you think's wrong with her?" asked Mum. "Do you think her brain's gone wonky?"

"There's nothing wonky with my brain," I said, annoyed.

"Let Doctor Cronk be the judge of that, Flo," said Mum.

"Indeed," said Doctor Cronk. "I'm highly trained in germs."

He removed my glasses and shone a bright light into my eyes and up my nose.

"Has she been overdoing it?" asked Doctor Cronk. "At school?"

"No," I said. "I've been talking to a lady in blue with exploding stars around her head."

Mum looked worried.

"Oh, what's to be done with her, Doctor?"

"Pills," said Dr Cronk. "Your daughter is highly strung. I want her to cut out eating chocolate and take a pink pill in the morning and a green pill at night. The pills will sort her out."

"Thank you Doctor," said Mum.

"My pleasure," said Doctor Cronk. "After all, I'm highly trained in germs."

"Yes," said Mum, "you're a genius."

But I knew otherwise. I didn't need pills. There was nothing wrong with me. I wasn't seeing a ghost. I was seeing a lady in blue (with exploding stars around her head). I needed to find George, quick. He'd back me up. George was in this, too. He'd prove I wasn't mad.

CHAPTER 9

Peculiar

"Well, I don't believe our Flo is mad," said Gran. "A lot of children have imaginary friends. I had one myself when I was a little girl. A tom cat called Sidney. I used to feed him invisible pilchards under the table. It did no harm."

"It's got to stop," said Mum. "All this talk of a woman hovering over the chip shop with no shoes on her feet. It's unhygienic."

Mum was in the kitchen making a pot of tea. She poked her head around the living room door.

"I don't want to hear another word about a lady in blue with exploding stars around her head. It's too creepy for comfort."

"Yes it is," said George.

I thought, what's George up to? He should be backing me up, not agreeing with Mum.

Mum went back into the kitchen. The kettle was blowing.

"Why did she have exploding stars around her head?" asked Gran. "Isn't that highly inflammable? She might set her hair alight and cause a fire."

"Don't encourage her," said Mum, walking back into the living room with a pot of tea and a plate of biscuits. "The lady in blue doesn't exist. She lives in our Flo's imagination."

"She does exist," I said. "Doesn't she, George?"

George said nothing. He pretended he hadn't heard. He was stuffing himself with biscuits. I was annoyed. I wanted him to

14

speak up. But then, I heard something (very mystifying and peculiar).

"I will show them a sign, dear. Proof I'm here."

It was the lady in blue, talking (crystal clear, inside my head).

I looked at George. He was rubbing one of his ears, like he'd got wax in it. I knew George could hear what I could hear. He was amazed.

"Let's drink our tea," said Mum. "and put all this talk of seeing blue weird women behind us."

"Yes," said Gran "I'm thirsty."

Mum and Gran began drinking their tea.

"The butcher's been flirting with me again," said Gran.

"Really?" said Mum.

"Yes. He's asked me out to the pictures, and yesterday he gave me a complimentary pound of sausages."

"Things like that can lead to allsorts," said Mum. "You want to be careful."

"That's true," said Gran. "But he's got a lovely moustache."

CHAPTER 10

Spooky

Gran finished drinking her tea and placed the cup onto her saucer.
I noticed Gran looking at something. She seemed shocked.
"Oh, would you look at this?" she cried. "In the bottom of my
teacup. How spooky."
"What is it?" asked Mum.
"There's a face appeared."
"A face?"
"Yes. It's the face of a woman, made up of tea leaves."
I quickly got up and looked into Gran's tea cup.

Guess what?

"It's her," I screamed. "Look, George." I held the teacup out for
George to see. He looked inside. The lady's face (made up from
tea leaves) smiled back! George quickly turned away.
"This is going too far, Flo," he said.
"Now will you believe me?" I said to Mum. "It's a sign."
"A sign of what?" said Mum, snatching the tea cup away.
"Proof," I said.
Mum stood staring into the teacup. She didn't say a word. She
just stared and stared.
"I'm off," said George, nervously. "I've got to go."
"Go where?" I said.
"Home."
"What for?"

"I can hear Dad calling me through the wall."

"No you can't."

George was lying.

"Yes I can," he said. "Dad wants me."

George stood up and quickly ran from the room. What's the matter with him?" I thought. Why's he acting like this?

"There's definitely a woman's face in the bottom of my teacup," said Gran. "Made up from tea leaves."

Mum kept on staring. Her brain working overtime, trying to work everything out. She kept blinking, and looking, blinking and looking. Then she looked at me, amazed, and shouted, "Let's telephone the local newspaper. Quick! This is big news."

CHAPTER 11

Flash

"I want you to look inside the teacup," said the photographer, "and imagine you're seeing the lady's face for the first time."

"Righto," said Mum, excited.

"I want faces of wonder," said the photographer.

"Righto," said Gran.

"Play our cards right," said the photographer, "and this story will make the front page of tonight's Evening Chronicle."

"Oh, I do hope so," said Mum. "I've always wanted to be famous."

"Pity you haven't got a dog," said the journalist (standing next to the photographer).

"Why?" asked Mum.

"Children, old people, mums, and dogs, always make the front page of the newspaper."

"Why?" I asked.

"Heart-warming," said the journalist.

"I've got a hamster," I said hopefully. "Would a hamster help?"

"It's better than nothing," said the journalist. "Go and fetch it."

I went to Bert's cage. He was sleeping. I woke Bert up and took him over to Mum and Gran.

"Dangle it over the teacup," said the photographer.

"Make it look astonished."

I didn't know how I was supposed to make Bert do that. I held Bert in both hands and let him peep into the teacup. Bert went all sleepy eyed and yawned. "Hurry up," said Mum, "I'm getting cramp in my fingers holding this tea cup."

"Ready?" said the photographer. "On the count of three. Faces of wonder. One, two, three."

Flash.

CHAPTER 12

Peeping

The photographer took our photo.

"So far so good," said the journalist. "Let's get on with the interview. You first saw the lady in blue sitting up a tree, you say?"

"Yes."

"And the next time was?"

"Hovering over the chip shop."

"Inside my telly," said Mum.

"And what did she say to you, Flo?" asked the journalist.

"The lady in blue said she was my friend. George saw her, too."

"Who's George?" asked the journalist.

"George lives next door."

"Oh, that's a nice touch," said the journalist.

"Go and fetch him. A little love interest always helps a story along."

"George isn't my boyfriend," I said.

"Do as you're told," said Mum. "This journalist knows her job, Flo, and I want my photograph in the newspaper." Mum smiled at the journalist. "You will say I'm only 39, won't you?"

I went next door to find George. I rang his doorbell, there was no answer. George wasn't there. At least I thought he wasn't there, until I saw him peeping through his bedroom curtains. George was hiding. His behaviour was becoming more and more peculiar? What was he up to? I went back home, annoyed.

CHAPTER 13

Slammed

The next evening, we couldn't believe it. Our photograph was on the front page of the newspaper!

"Oh, it's the spitting image of me," Mum cried. "Don't I look gorgeous?"

"Oh yes," I said.

The only downside was, the story got Mum's age wrong. Instead of saying she was 39, it said Mum was 93! It was a misprint (I think).

It was really good to read about us in the newspaper. But I was puzzled about something? The newspaper headline said,

"MARY'S FACE APPEARS IN TEACUP"

How did they know her name? I didn't know her name was Mary?

The Evening Chronicle seemed to know more about the lady in blue than I did. Who said she was called Mary? She could have been called Gladys for all I knew. I went round to George's house again. He hadn't been in school. I hadn't seen him all day. I wanted to show him the newspaper story. I pressed his door bell, nobody answered. I knocked the knocker, but nobody came, so I pushed the newspaper through the letter box, and left. Five minutes later, George turned up on our doorstep and he wasn't pleased. He was furious.

"Why did you talk to the newspaper?" he shouted. "Why did you say I was in love with you, and hoped we'd get married?"

"I didn't say I was in love with you, and I never mentioned anything about marriage. The newspaper made it up."

"Why did you mention us both seeing the lady in blue?

"Well, we did see her."

"No I didn't."

I was amazed. What was George going on about?

"Dad says I didn't see anything."

"Oh really?" I said.

"Yes. Dad says I should grow up and stop being soft. Dad doesn't want me to play with you again."

"But… George?"

He wouldn't listen. George ran back to his house and slammed the front door

SHUT.

BANG.

I was gobsmacked!

CHAPTER 14

Freak

The next day, George still wasn't in school, so when I got back home, I knelt down and shouted through his letter box.

"We did see her, George. You know we did."

"Bog off!"

It was George's dad. He opened the front door and looked at me, drunk. He was really mad. He wore a dirty vest, and stained trousers. His eyes were red and his fingernails were filthy. He was grubby all over. SWEATY.

"Hop it!" he shouted.

"What?"

"You heard me. Freak."

I didn't understand.

"Who's a… freak?"

"You are. Mary's face appears in a tea cup? Have you gone daft?" he slurred. "What a load of… flipping… tripe" (he was almost swearing!).

I wanted to say, why are you calling me names? I'm not a freak. But I didn't, because I could see George peering through his bedroom window. And he looked very frightened.

"Don't upset him," he shouted. "Please, Flo, not while he's drinking. Dad breaks things. Leave us both alone."

I felt sorry for George and went back home. Sometimes parents can be a bit troublesome, can't they? Especially a dad who's drunk.

CHAPTER 15

Lonely

Later on, when I told Gran about George telling me to leave, she explained, I'd got to understand that George's dad was still getting over his wife's death. Gran said he was feeling upset. Perhaps he was a little jealous of me and George spending our time together. Perhaps his dad wanted George to spend more time with him.

"When someone dies," Gran said, "you feel very sad, and lonely, especially if it's your wife."

I'm sure Gran was right. I really hoped George and me would be friends again. But I couldn't help feeling let down by him, big time. George was supposed to be my best friend. We played all sorts of games together - Ghosts, Queens, Pirates, and Kings. There was always lots of brilliant things to do. George and me would magic up stories. Every day. And now we couldn't. George had stopped playing, and I felt sad.

CHAPTER 16

Gift

The next morning, still no George. I went to school on my own again. Well, that's what I thought, until…

"Good morning."

It was her, the lady in blue, sitting next to me on the 39 bus!

"Hello," I said. "What you doing here?"

"I've come to see you."

I couldn't believe it. One minute she wasn't there, the next minute she was!

"Are you real?" I asked.

"I beg pardon?"

"George says you don't exist."

"I'm as real as this morning's birdsong," said the lady in blue, laughing (her laugh sounded like little tinkling bells).

"Good, then I'm not going mad."

"Who thinks you're mad?"

I didn't answer.

I wanted to ask her something about the newspaper story.

"Is your name Mary?"

"Yes, of course. Didn't you know?"

"No. I know nothing about you."

An old man was listening to everything, sat behind us. He smelt of onions. I needed to ask Mary some more things.

"The newspaper said you're a mother. Is that true?"

"Yes, that's true," Mary smiled.

I liked her smile. It was friendly. The more Mary spoke to me, the more I liked her. I thought, she can't be a ghost. She must be something else. Something nice…

But what?

The bus stopped and the old man stood up.

"Who are you talking to?" he asked.

"Mother Mary," I said.

"Don't be cheeky," he said, "A smart answer for everything, kids nowadays. Think you're clever don't you, making fun of the elderly?"

I didn't answer back. What did he know? He couldn't see what I could see. He couldn't see I was talking to an invisible lady wearing a blue dress and a blue scarf around her head (she looked like someone you see from the olden days. A different time).

"Look here," said Mary, "I want you to have this. A gift."

I couldn't believe it. I hadn't a clue where she'd got it. One minute her hand was empty, then…

It was there,
A rose.

The most beautiful rose
I'd seen in my life.

"Oh thank you," I said. "How lovely."

I looked around to see if anybody else could see. But nobody could see anything. The people on the bus looked like they were dead. They were just thinking about going to work and miserable stuff like that.

"Why can't anybody else see you, Mary?" I asked.

"They can," said Mary. "If they want, but most people prefer not."

"Why?"

"Nowadays… all the mystery has gone."

I didn't know what Mary meant, and before I could ask her any more, she did it again. Mary vanished. In a flash! A blue flash!

"Oh, please don't go."

But she'd gone. It was like Mary had never been there at all.

But in my hand, something remained.

My gift, from Mary.
The beautiful rose,
and it was the colour…

blue.

CHAPTER 17

Trash

"Here she comes," said Julie, "our local celebrity." Julie was pretending she didn't care about my photograph being in the newspaper. But I could tell she was jealous. I walked past her. Miss Tickle stood at the classroom door, putting on her lipstick.

"Where do you think you're going?"

"I'm going to my desk, Miss," I said.

"Oh no you're not. You've an appointment with the headmistress."

"And she's not pleased," smirked Julie. "Ha."

I could tell Miss Cathcart was in a bad mood as soon as I got into her office. Her dangly earrings (big brass conkers) always wobbled when she was annoyed. And today they were twirling like golf balls. I thought Miss Cathcart's dangly earrings might explode.

"What are you up to?" she cried. "All this talk about… Mother Mary! It's ridiculous. I can't have you telling the whole of Manchester you've seen a religious icon in a tea cup!"

"A religious what?"

"My school can't be seen to favour one religion over any other. We have Muslims, Sikhs, Buddhists, allsorts here. The school governors will go bananas."

"I don't understand."

"You're a liar," said Miss Cathcart.

"Well, George Roper in Class 4 saw her, too," I said.

"No he didn't. I've just spoken to George on the telephone, and he's convinced you put the idea into his head, playing. You're an attention seeker, Florence Hargreaves, and it's got to stop."

Miss Cathcart was not pleased. She was so mad that one of her earrings shot off, flew through the air and landed in a fish tank.

PLOP.

Tropical fish swam about, darting everywhere, like a bomb had gone off.

SPLASH.

"Right" said Miss Cathcart (removing plastic seaweed from her blouse), "I want you to tell me the truth. What are you playing at?"

"Nothing," I said.

"Then you'll leave this school today!" cried Miss Cathcart. "And not come back until you're willing to admit you're nothing but a story teller. A LIAR!"

"I won't," I said.

"Get out!" cried Miss Cathcart.

I was really upset.

Why would nobody believe me?

What harm was I doing?

I started to walk from Miss Cathcart's office, there was no point in arguing. Her mind was made up. Miss Cathcart didn't believe in the lady in blue, and that was that.

But then, I suddenly remembered something.

"Look at this," I said.

I took from my schoolbag....

The blue rose.

"She gave it me," I said.
"Who did?" asked Miss Cathcart.
"Mary. She gave me the rose this morning on the 39 bus."
Miss Cathcart wasn't impressed. Her other earring started twirling (violently).
"Do you think I was born yesterday?" she hissed. "A rose like that can be purchased from any cheap petrol station."
"Not like this," I said. "It's… blue."
"It's painted blue."
"It's a magical blue."
"It's COMMON," shouted Miss Cathcart "You get them free with petrol tokens."
"It's a very special gift." I cried.
"GEEEEEEEEET OUT!" screamed Miss Cathcart." You're talking TRASH."

CHAPTER 18

Sad

It was obvious Miss Cathcart was never going to believe me.
She'd forgotten how to believe. At forty years old (could be fifty)
she would never believe in anything magical again. So I just
walked away, out through the school gates, and felt sorry for her.

Mary's rose was never common.
It was… beautiful.

I explained the whole thing to Gran when I got to her laundrette.
"What a cheek," said Gran. "How dare Miss Cathcart say you're a
story teller. I know what I saw in that teacup and it was a
woman's face."
Gran was annoyed for me. She quickly put the 'Closed' sign up
on the launderette door and reached for her coat.
"Come with me," she said. "I want to show you something."
"Where we going?"
"All will be revealed," said Gran, mysteriously. "Come on."

CHAPTER 19

Happiness

We walked over the road, where the wild weeds grow. It's called "The Dirt Tip". We kept on walking until we arrived at a very old building. The building's windows were smashed and boarded up a long time ago. A big sign said, 'For Sale'. The building looked haunted. Like a very old, crumbling palace.

"They want to sell this place and turn it into luxury flats," said Gran. "Me and your granddad used to come here. It was a beautiful place back then. Quite beyond the imagination."

I never knew my granddad. He died from a bad cold before I was born. We entered the building. It was very dark, the colour of grey and silver with bits of black. I could hear pigeons cooing somewhere high up in the roof. You had to be very careful. It was a land of bird dirt and rotting carpets. There was a faint smell of a very old perfume. A sort of musty, but sweet smell. Gran called it 'frankincense'. She walked to a table and put some money into an old wooden box.

"It pays for the candles," she said.

Gran took hold of a candle, and lit the candle from one of the others, burning on a stand. Gran crossed herself and did a little curtsy to a man with nails in his hands and feet. He had a crown of sticks on his head. He looked really fed up and sad. He was a statue.

"Who's that?" I said.

"Jesus." said Gran. "Don't they teach you anything at school?"

"No," I said.

We walked down a strip of faded purple carpet. It led into a stone room. The walls looked damp, stained, flaky with peeling paint. "Look," said Gran, "that's her, isn't it?"

I looked at a painting on the wall. It was very old and faded. I went all funny in my tummy. She looked the same, only sort of different, but I could tell it was her. She had the same stars spinning around her head, and she wore a long dress with no shoes. It was the same face, the same eyes and the same smile. She was hovering over the world. Like a fairy queen. And her dress was…

blue.

"Well?" said Gran. "What do you say?"
I said nothing. I just kept looking at the painting. Gran smiled at me.
"I knew it," said Gran. "You've been visited by someone special, and don't let anyone tell you different."
I began to smile. I felt happy. I looked at Gran and down her cheek saw a tiny little tear. It sparkled in the candlelight. Like a tiny little star. But I could tell Gran wasn't sad. She was happy like me. The painting made us both feel good. Gran held her candle up close to the painting. Under the painting was a small brass plaque, on the plaque, was the name of the painting.
The painting was called

"Our Lady. Mary".

It was at that moment, something amazing happened. A perfume. A fragrance. Floating all around me. It was… like the smell… of… happiness.

And I knew,
it was the perfume
of her rose,

Mary's rose,

the blue rose,

and the perfume
was so…
beautiful,

I felt dizzy,
and suddenly...
I wanted to…

dance.

And so I did. Me and Gran held our hands together and we slowly danced around the falling down building. Gran said the dance was called a waltz. And so we both waltzed together, smiling, while Mary in her painting watched. And the pigeons began to sing, "coo coo cooooooooo." It was great.

"What is this mysterious place called, Gran?" I asked.

"Well," said Gran, "today they call it 'a condemned building' but when I was young, I married your grandfather here, and they called it a church… The Church of Our Lady."

CHAPTER 20

Proof

"We'll put the rose, here." said Gran, "in my laundrette window. And we'll put a sign up, saying, 'Mary's Rose'. That way, anybody who says she didn't come to visit you, will see the rose and say, here's the proof."

"Good idea," I said.

We put the rose in a jam jar with some tap water and placed it in the window with a sign:

'MARY'S ROSE'
'The proof'

I wrote the sign myself, in felt tip.

"Now, let's have something to eat," said Gran. "All that dancing has made me famished. I've got a big custard tart in the fridge, lets share it."

"Oh, great, Gran."

And that's what we did. Two slices each. With cream. It was delicious. I love my gran.

CHAPTER 21

Chuffed

When I got home and told mum and dad I'd been thrown out of school, they didn't seem bothered.

"Never mind," said Mum.

"Who cares," said Dad.

They both started jumping up and down on the sofa. They didn't seem mad. They seemed excited.

"What's up with you?" I said.

"We've had a phone call," said Dad. "We're going on the telly."

"The telly?" I said (amazed).

"Yes," cried Mum, "we're going on the Gloria Riccardo Talk Show. She wants you to talk about Mary."

"Oooooooooooh," I said, "that's amazing."

"Yes," cried Mum, "isn't it fabulous? Me and your dad are both chuffed."

CHAPTER 22

Make-up

Gloria Riccardo didn't look anything like she did on the telly, not without her make-up. She didn't look shiny or glossy. She looked dry and crumbly. Thank goodness for Vera. It was Vera's job to make Gloria's face look like a television star. Which wasn't easy. It was hard work. Vera spent hours making up Gloria's face, and all the time, Gloria kept giving him a slap, and shouting,
"I don't look glamorous enough. Try harder. Fool."
Poor Vera. He was a nervous wreck.

After Vera finished doing Gloria's make up, he stuck a big blonde wig on her head. The wig was gigantic (like a haystack). The wig did the trick. It made Gloria look exactly like the famous TV star everyone knew.
"That's me done," said Gloria, admiring herself in the mirror. "See you later on the set, darlings." Gloria left the make-up room, spraying herself with perfume – 'Glamour Toilette.'

Vera patted the make-up chair.
"Your turn," he said.
I sat down. Vera removed my glasses and started rubbing pink stuff onto my cheeks. He powdered my face in some peach colour, and made my eyelashes look nice and long. Next, he tied my hair back with a big pink ribbon.
"There," said Vera. "You look much better."
I looked in the mirror. I looked about five years old!

"I don't look anything like me," I said.

"Of course not. We don't want you to look like you," said Vera. "The telly viewers don't want to see an ordinary girl with untidy hair. They want to see someone sweet and lovely. You've got to have the correct image to appear on TV."

Vera held up the make-up tin.

"Peaches and Cream," he said.

"Oh, doesn't Flo look lovely," Mum preened. "I wouldn't have known it was her. She looks like peaches and cream."

I wasn't sure I wanted to look like 'peaches and cream'. Vera was pleased.

"Sit yourself down," Vera said to Mum. "Your turn next."

Mum sat down.

"Oh goodie," she said, "I can't wait."

"First…" said Vera, "I'm going to apply a little gel and work it through these curls in your hair."

"Don't you like my new hair-do?" said Mum. "I've had it done especially."

"Your hair looks lovely," said Vera, "but I'm afraid it's not the right image for the telly. The producer wants you to look like a real working mum, not a party girl."

"But I am a real mum," said Mum.

"Trust me," said Vera, "When I've finished with you, you'll look just right."

Mum closed her eyes and sat back in the make-up chair.

"Do your business, Vera," she said, "I'm in your professional hands."

It didn't take Vera long to work his make-up magic. In fact, it only took a matter of minutes.

"You can open your eyes now," said Vera.

"Righto," said Mum.

I could tell Mum was excited.

"What do you think?" asked Vera "Do you like it?"

Mum looked into the mirror.

"Ahhhhhhhhhhhhhhh!" she screamed "What have you done to me? My hair's tangled up like a wet dog, I've big dark circles under my eyes. I look terrible. Worn out."

"Precisely," said Vera. "That's exactly how you're supposed to look." Vera held up the tin of make-up he'd slapped onto Mum's face. 'Worn out Woman' the tin said.

"I don't want to look worn out," cried Mum, "I want to look gorgeous."

"That's not the part you're here to play," said Vera.

"I don't want to play a part, I want to be me."

"Everybody plays a part on TV, silly."

"What about me?" asked Dad. "Do I have to wear make-up?"

"Of course," said Vera,

Dad didn't look very pleased.

All this talk of make-up, and having to change the way you look. It was like being a real person wasn't good enough for TV. It seemed you had to pretend to be somebody else, someone the TV people wanted you to be. I found this a bit confusing and a bit strange.

I watched Vera put make-up onto Dad's face.

It said on the make-up tin, 'Angry Man'.

Is that Dad's part?" I asked.

"Yes" said Vera. "Doesn't he look frightening? Come on, you're all made up and ready to play your parts. It's time to go on 'The Gloria Riccardo TV show'. Follow me."

CHAPTER 23

Television

A red light flashed, 'Transmission'. The Gloria Riccardo TV show started. It felt exciting!

Gloria asked me about Mary (live on TV), "How many times have you seen her?" She asked me about George, "Why aren't you seeing him anymore?" She asked me about school, "Why has Miss Cathcart, the head mistress, sent you home?"

I told Gloria everything. The TV audience applauded and the interview felt good. Next, Mum was asked how she was coping with the news of me seeing 'Mary'?

"Are you worried?" asked Gloria, concerned.

"Well…" said Mum, "I… suppose… if…"

"Did you hear that, ladies and gentlemen," said Gloria, "this mother is… worried. And who cares about a mother's worries? Nobody."

Gloria looked into the TV camera, cross. It was like she was talking to every person sat at home.

"I hope you're satisfied with your actions, Miss Cathcart."

The audience applauded. They agreed with Gloria.

"You've ruined this mother's life! Look at her! She's WORN OUT!"

Gloria spoke to my dad next.

"I bet you'd like to… give Miss Cathcart a good THUMP."

Well… er…" Dad said, "I… suppose… if…"

"Violence," said Gloria, "will never get to the heart of a family's problems."

Gloria sat down next to Dad. Her voice went all warm and treacly. She took hold of his hand, caringly.

"Would you like to talk to a family counsellor?" she purred.

"Why?" said Dad, confused.

"To rid yourself of anger?"

The TV audience shouted:

"Yes... Yes... GET SOME HELP!"

Gloria fluttered her eyelashes at Dad more caringly.

"Would you like me to sort out your family's problems?"

What problems?

"Er well..." said Dad, "I... suppose... if..."

"Good," said Gloria, "I'll arrange it. Look at this ANGRY MAN, everyone! He needs my help."

The audience cheered. Gloria smiled.

"Thank you... thank you," she said, touching her heart. "I'm here to help everybody... Help is the name of the game... on the Gloria Riccardo Show. ...Time for a commercial break."

CHAPTER 24

Scared

I looked at the TV monitor. I could see the words, 'End of Part One'. I could see commercials being shown, advertising toilet rolls and deodorants. It was very interesting being on TV.

"Time for my touch up," Gloria shouted, "MAKE-UP!"
Vera quickly appeared from behind a camera. He started to comb and spray Gloria's big wig.
"Hurry up you fool," hissed Gloria, "make me look more glamorous, the commercial break is nearly over."

Red lights flashed – 'Transmission'.

"Part 2" began.

"Welcome back, darlings," Gloria said, smiling. "And now we come to the part of my show where we get to the heart of the family's big problem."

A TV camera zoomed into my face.

"Florence Hargreaves," said Gloria, "let's have it."
The TV audience looked at me. Their faces seemed cross.
A BIG HUSH

What was happening?

I didn't know what was going on. I just stared at Gloria, bewildered, and said nothing.

"Don't play gormless, said Gloria. (Her voice sounded hard, not friendly). "It's time to tell everybody in TV land the truth. Why are you making up stories about seeing Mother Mary?"

Oh my Goodness!

"I'm not making up stories," I said, nervously.

"Don't play the little innocent with me," said Gloria. "I wasn't born yesterday. Perhaps you don't get enough love at home? Is that why you crave attention?"

What was Gloria talking about?

"Or perhaps," said Gloria, "you're just a calculating little girl, who knows what she's up to, and is willing to make up any story, just so she can be on national television and make herself famous, like me."

"I'm… I'm… not making anything up," I said.

"Then…" shouted Gloria, "bring out the LIE DETECTOR."

The audience went wild. A man wearing a white coat (like some kind of brain surgeon) walked into the TV studio pushing a big silver box, a machine, with flashing green and yellow lights, electric wires and things. I looked at Mum and Dad. They both seemed worried.

The audience went bonkers. Whooping and cheering. The man in the white coat stuck the coloured wires onto my fingers and placed a metal helmet on my head.

"Is that safe?" asked Mum.

"Yes," said Gloria, "if your daughter is telling the truth."

"Are you ready?" said Gloria.

I said nothing. I was frightened.

"Very well, turn on the LIE DETECTOR."

The man in the white coat pressed a button and the machine began to make a soft, purring sound (like a cat when it's going to jump on a mouse). I was feeling really scared (the wires stuck onto my fingers were glowing hot).

"Right," said Gloria, "What I want to know is this…" Gloria looked at me, like she was an evil witch. "Did you really see Mother Mary, a religious icon, sat up a tree? True or false?"

"True," I said.

The TV audience gasped.

"Very well," said Gloria, "turn the Lie Detector 'full on'."

"Here we go," said the man in the white coat.

He turned a big dial. Lights flashed, a bell rang, a buzzer buzzed, and a horn honked three times. A card flew out of the machine.

'Ping!'

The man in the white coat took hold of the card and handed it to Gloria. The audience leaned forward trying to read it.

"I have the data here," said Gloria. "I asked this little girl, if she'd seen Mother Mary sat up a tree, and her answer was…

"True" I said.

Gloria looked into the TV camera. Her face seemed very serious (like a policewoman). "The lie detector says...

FALSE!"

"Oooooooooooooooooooooooooooooooooooooooooooooooooooooh," cried the TV audience.
"She's a liar," cried Gloria.
"A liar!"

CHAPTER 25

Liar

"Liar! Liar!" cried the TV audience.

"Oh Florence," cried Mum.

"Oh Florence," said Dad.

"How could you?" cried Vera.

"The game is up," said Gloria. "Admit you're a LIAR! You never saw Mother Mary!"

"…I did see her," I said (I was burning up, confused). "I did see her, and she gave me something."

"What? said Gloria

"A rose."

"A rose?"

"Yes, a blue rose. It's in my gran's laundrette."

Gloria wasn't interested in Gran's launderette.

"Poppycock!" She cried. "Come on, admit you're a fibber."

"No," I said. "Why should I? I don't care about your stupid lie detector. I know what the truth is. And…"

Then something happened.

It was a strange and peculiar feeling. Almost a giddy feeling. Like when you twirl around too much and stop too sudden and fall over. It was like when your body goes one way and your mind is left somewhere else (swivelling).

I heard a voice…

speaking
inside
my head.

Talking
to me,
inside my head.

It was… Mary!

It felt like magic, inside my brain, like a meadow of fresh brand new flowers was springing up and growing everywhere.

I started to speak, not sure what I was saying (I sounded like a robot). "Look up into the sky this evening. Mary will show you a sign," I said.
"A sign?" said Gloria, "what kind of a sign?"
"A sign to show… Mary's here. Proof."

"Ahhhhhhhhhhhhhhhhhhhhhhhhhhhhhhhhhhhhh," I suddenly screamed.

Blackout.

After that I don't remember anything. I just sort of… passed out.

CHAPTER 26

Jealous

Blackness.

When I came to, I was in the TV make-up room. Mum and Dad were wafting me with a towel.

"Thank Goodness, she's alive," said Mum, "I thought she'd burst a blood vessel or something."

Gloria sat watching, drinking a large glass of whisky and eating a meat pie. She didn't look very pleased.

"What an act!" she hissed. "Oh What a performance! I've got to hand it to you, little girl, I didn't expect this. You stole my show. The whole country will be staring up into the sky this evening. And everybody will be talking about YOU! and not ME!"

Gloria swigged her glass of whiskey back in one go, and burped.

Oh dear!

She was fuming. I'd stolen her show. Gloria wasn't pleased at all. She was jealous!

CHAPTER 27

Sniff

Later, me and Gran started folding up washing in her laundrette.

"She called me a liar," I said, "live on TV."

"Try not to worry," said Gran. "If people don't want to believe the truth, you can't make them."

"The lie detector didn't believe me, either," I said.

"What does that prove?" said Gran. "There's not a machine built on earth that can detect if something is mystical or not."

I didn't know what Gran meant. I knew Gran was usually right about lots of things. And there were still lots of things about Mary I didn't understand, so I said, "Why is everybody getting mad at me, Gran, because I can see Mary?"

"Well," said Gran, "Mary is a very important person She doesn't appear to everybody. She's special. The mother of Jesus."

"Jesus?"

"Yes. You saw him in church, remember? His statue?"

"The man with sticks on his head?"

"Yes. A crown of thorns."

"I don't know anything about him, Gran."

"You know his story, it's in the Bible.

"I don't."

"He was killed."

"Killed?" I was shocked. "Why was he killed?"

"Some people didn't like him."

I didn't know what to say. Poor Mary. Her son was killed, and I never knew. Before I could ask Gran any more about it, the laundrette door opened and a young woman entered, pushing an old woman in a wheelchair. It was old Mrs Zandy and her daughter, Zulema.

Zulema opened a washing bag and started putting knickers, pairs of tights, and bras, into a washing machine. While this was happening, I noticed old Mrs Zandy starting to sniff the air like a rabbit. Her nose wriggled.

Sniff.
Sniff.
Sniff.

"What's that smell?" she said.

"Well, it's not me, mother," said Zulema.

"Oh, it smells beautiful," said Mrs Zandy, "I think its… coming from that blue rose in the window."

"I can't smell anything," said Zulema, "I've a cold."

I looked at Gran. I could tell Gran could smell something. Her nose was twitching too.

Sniff.
Sniff.
Sniff.

"Ignore mother," said Zulema, "she's 99 and lives in a fantasy world."

"I'm telling you I can smell something pungent in the air, and it's coming from that blue rose."

I went to the window and took hold of Mary's rose. I held the rose up to my nose. And sniffed. The perfume was very strong (like blue hyacinths mixed with strawberries and fresh raindrops).

"Let me have a sniff," said Mrs Zandy. "Give the rose to me."

I gave Mrs Zandy the rose. She gave a great big sniff, and closed her eyes.

Snnnniiiiiffff.

"Oh, I feel… tingly. My fingers feel tingly, my toes feel tingly, my legs feel tingly and my feet feel tingly."

"Are you having a nasty turn, mother?"

"No," said Mrs Zandy. "I've never felt better in my life. Every time I get a whiff of this rose, I feel wonderful. It smells… like rhubarb and custard mixed with honey ice cream, and… its making me want to…"

Suddenly, Mrs Zandy's legs shot out in front of her.

"Oh heck!" cried Zulema. "What's happening?"

CHAPTER 28

Dancing

"I can't stop my legs wiggling," shouted Mrs Zandy. "Oh, my legs have got a life of their own."

Zulema quickly grabbed hold of her mother's legs. But she couldn't stop them wiggling. Her mother's legs were like elastic. Wiggling and wiggling around and around. You'd think she was riding a bicycle!

"Will you stop it, mother," cried Zulema. "You're showing the tops of your tights!"

But Mrs Zandy couldn't stop. Her legs wiggled more and more. Faster and faster. Then… Mrs Zandy suddenly started kicking high into the air, like she was a can-can dancer from Paris. She kicked, and she kicked, and she kicked, higher and higher and higher, knocking her daughter over.

THUMP.

"Ouch!"

Then… Mrs Zandy suddenly jumped out of her wheelchair.

"Yippee!"

"Oh, what's happening?" screamed Zulema in a panic.

"My legs have been given a new lease of life," said Mrs Zandy.

"Look, I'm… dancing!"

"No!" cried Zulema, in shock.

"It's bloomin' marvellous. I don't need to sit in my wheelchair anymore. It's the rose. It's making me dance. I want to…"

Suddenly, Mrs Zandy did a back flip.

"Aaaaaahhhhhhhh!" screamed Zulema

I thought she would pass out!

Me and Gran couldn't believe it. Mrs Zandy just laughed. She was so excited, she threw the rose into the air, and luckily I caught it.

"I'm filled to the brim with… electricity!"

And sure enough, you could see the electricity around Mrs Zandy's body. It was blue and whizzing and crackling. The more Mrs Zandy danced, the more the electricity flew off her legs. Electricity hit the washing machines, causing them to whirl faster and faster. Mrs Zandy kept on dancing and waving her skirt up and down. You could see blue sparks flying up and down her tights.

"Oh, Stop it! Stop it!" shrieked Zulema, "You're singeing your underskirt, mother!"

But Mrs Zandy couldn't stop (or wouldn't). She bent her knees and started wiggling her arms from side to side, then she started wiggling her backside.

HER BUM!

"Oh!" screamed Zulema. "Is your bum on fire?"

CHAPTER 29

Weeeeeee

"It's the hippie hippie shake!" laughed Mrs Zandy "A dance I used to do years ago when I was young and having fun."

Inside the washing machines you could see the washing tumbling faster and faster. The washing seemed to be glowing, brighter and brighter. Everything seemed more alive. Whizzing, brilliant… blue.

"Weeeeeeee!" shouted Mrs Zandy, opening the laundrette's door.

"Where you going?" cried Zulema.

"I'm going to dance down the street and find myself a fella."

"Oh no you're not, Mother! Come back here."

But it was too late. Mrs Zandy leapt out of the laundrette and started dancing down the street. Zulema ran after her, but she couldn't catch up. Mrs Zandy was dancing far too fast. Arms and legs waving like an electrified octopus. The last we saw of Mrs Zandy, she was leaping and prancing into a local pub called "THE GOLDEN GOOSE (men started cheering).

"I blame you for this," screamed Zulema.

"It's not our fault," cried Gran. "It was the rose that did it."

"Rubbish," shouted Zulema. "I didn't smell a thing."

But it was true. The blue rose had caused everything.

It was then, I noticed something else happening. Something very mysterious. The most extraordinary thing of all. There were lots of people standing in the street, and everyone was looking upwards into the evening sky. Some stood at open windows, others sat looking up from inside their cars. And everybody had the same look on their faces.

A look of wonder.

It was very eerie.

There was peace and quiet.

A big hush.

Nobody was talking.

It seemed in that moment,
a silence
was everywhere
in the world.

Nobody could believe
what they were…
seeing.

I couldn't believe it, and neither could Gran.

It was... Amazing.

"Oh, it's a miracle," said Gran, staring up into the stars."
"Oh look," I said.

"The moon… is… blue."

CHAPTER 30

Awesome

"A strange thing happened this evening," said the newsreader. "Millions of people throughout the world have witnessed the moon turning blue."

At this point the television news started showing a clip of the Gloria Riccardo Show. It was the bit about me and the lie detector, and Gloria asking about Mary, and me saying I'd seen her up in a tree and the lie detector saying I hadn't, and the audience shouting "Liar…" and me getting upset and talking like a robot, and saying,

"Mary will show you a sign. Proof."

Then, the television news started showing pictures of the moon
changing
colour.

The moon
turning
blue.

Oh!

There were thousands of people watching it around the world, and their faces looked ghostly in the blue moonlight. It was awesome. And some people started saying they could see a woman's face in the blue moon. While others said, no, it was only the moon's shadow, craters, mountains, and things, causing optical illusions. But whatever people were seeing, it affected them massively. Some of them started falling down onto their knees, and one or two began to sing (hymns). And then, the newsreader came back on the telly, and sitting next to him was Gloria Riccardo in a massive wig (the size of a hot air balloon!).

"What do you think is happening here, Gloria?" said the newsreader.

"Well, something very mysterious is happening, indeed."

"Do you think your Lie Detector got it wrong?"

I could tell Gloria was trying to squirm her way out of it.

"My lie detector is always a hundred per cent right," said Gloria, "and never gets anything wrong. But… nothing in the world is perfect, is it?"

"Are you saying this little girl, Florence Hargreaves, who appeared on your TV programme, might be telling the truth?"

"Well…" said Gloria twitching.

"Don't pussyfoot around Gloria," said the newsman, "I want a straight answer. This is a news programme, not a light entertainment show. Do you believe Florence Hargreaves is telling the truth? Did she see Mother Mary, a religious icon to millions, floating over a chip shop in Manchester or not?"

"Well…" said Gloria, "a blue moon doesn't happen every evening, does it? So, there is more to this story than meets the eye."

"Perhaps a miracle?" said the newsreader.

"God knows!" said Gloria." How should I know? I'm a telly star. Not a nun."

I went to bed feeling really really good. There was more to my story than "meets the eye." Gloria Riccardo had said so on the TV news!

Awesome.

CHAPTER 31

Fantastic

"Thanks Mary," I said (inside my head).

"Don't mention it, dear."

"Is that you, Mary?" I said, sitting up in bed.

"Of course, Florence, who do you think it is? Father Christmas?"

I looked around my bedroom. I couldn't see anyone. Just shadows.

"Where are you?"

"I'm over here," said Mary

"Over where?"

"The other side of the world, dear."

"And you can hear me?"

"Yes. Of course."

I thought this was an amazing thing to do without a phone.

"How can you do that?" I asked.

"I just… listen very carefully," said Mary.

I was impressed.

"What you doing the other side of the world?"

"Well, at this precise moment, I'm having a cup of tea with the Blue Buddha. Do you know him?"

"No," I said. "Is he nice?"

"Very. He's my friend."

I realised I didn't understand that much about anything. I didn't know anything about the world, except where I lived. My life was ordinary. I hadn't a clue about Mary's life. I knew nothing about her, really, and nothing about her son. If Mary was a very important person, why should she want to talk with me? A girl that just lives in an old house that's waiting to be knocked down? It's not like I was rich and lived on the new development like Julie or anything.

"Why are you doing this?" I asked

"Doing what?" said Mary

"Appearing in my head and telling me things."

"Well," said Mary, "it's nice to get to know someone new, isn't it, being friends?"

"Yes," I said.

"Good," Mary said, "It makes the world much more colourful."

"Like turning the moon blue?" I asked.

Mary just laughed, "Perhaps?"

Outside, far away, an old clock chimed somewhere. It was late. I was tired and started to yawn. I wanted to ask Mary more about her son (him being killed, like Gran said), but I didn't know how to bring him up, and I was sleepy. It had been a long, exciting day, what with the moon turning blue and my story making the TV news.

"I think you're tired," said Mary.

"I think I am."

"Goodnight, Flo."

"Goodnight, Mary."

"Shubha raatri."

(it was a man's voice).

"Who's that?" I said, surprised

"The Blue Buddha," said Mary. "Sweet dreams."

"Pyare sapne." said the Blue Buddha.

"Pyare sapne," I said (whatever that meant?).

I didn't have to wait long to fall asleep and dream. It felt like I'd been dreaming already. My head was full of dreams. I was dreaming in my dreams! What a mystery my life was becoming. Each day seemed more and more…

fantastic.

CHAPTER 32

Explosion

"I can explain everything," said the man with a bald head. "What the world witnessed last night when the moon turned blue, was not a mystery. Our world is a sensible world, full of scientific facts."

"Rubbish," said Mum, eating toast.

"Rubbish," said Dad, slurping his tea.

The man talking on Breakfast TV wore a dickie bow. He was a scientist.

"It is my scientific opinion that magic does not happen anywhere nowadays. Magic belongs in the past. It belongs in fairy stories. This is a modern age. I will explain why the moon turned blue, and there is nothing unworldly about it. Last night a big explosion happened at a cake factory in Wigan, causing a great cloud of dust to blow up into the sky. Some people thought they'd seen a blue moon, but they hadn't. They'd seen a cloud of blue icing sugar, floating past the moon. It made the moon look like a blue, flying birthday cake."

"What a load of crap," said Dad.

"I don't believe a word," said Mum.

"It's a fact," said the scientist on the telly. "And a fact is a fact. So there."

CHAPTER 33

Money

I looked at the people standing in our living room. They started asking me questions about what the TV scientist had said. They were shouting and arguing. They were journalists from the national newspapers. Mum and Dad had let them into the house, because they said they wanted to buy my "Blue Moon story". They were bidding, with lots of money.

Mum and Dad were well pleased.

"Play our cards right," said Dad, "we'll get a nice holiday out of this."

"And new carpets," smiled Mum.

Dad started talking to one of the journalists alone, while the others kept shouting and bombarding me with blue moon questions. It was really rowdy. I had to cover up both my ears with cushions.

"Right, that's it," Dad shouted. "The Daily Rag is willing to pay five thousand pounds for my daughter's 'exclusive tale'… erm… 'true story'… and it's a deal."

The other journalists started moaning.

"Stop your moaning," cried Mum. "Go on, get out. You had your chance, and didn't bid high enough."

Dad didn't stand any messing (he used to lift weights before his hernia). He threw the complaining journalists out of the house, and when they'd gone, Dad started making a real fuss of me (which he'd never done before). It felt great.

"Sit yourself down, darling child," said Dad, "and tell this nice man from The Daily Rag your story."

I wasn't nervous about talking to the Rag man one bit, because Dad was being lovely to me. Most days he didn't really notice I was there. The Rag man asked me about Mary and George. He asked me about Miss Cathcart throwing me out of school, and he asked me about the Gloria Riccardo show and the lie detector and the blue moon. He wasn't very interested in what the scientist had said. He said nobody wants to read about facts with their cornflakes. He said the public wanted something mind blowing to read while eating their breakfast. They wanted to hear about me and magic, not about scientific rubbish. So, I told him about Mary's blue rose and about Mrs Zandy jumping out of her wheelchair and being able to dance.

"It was the rose that did it," I said. "One sniff, and Mrs Zandy could do 'the hippie hippie shake'."

"This story of yours," said the Rag man, "it's sensational. The magic gets bigger and better."

Mum and dad were smiling. I could tell they were really pleased with me. I felt so good. And I wondered if this feeling would carry on forever. The lady in blue was making my life feel wonderful. Happy Happy Happy.

CHAPTER 34

Snazzy

"How fortunate I am," said Dad, "to have such a precious daughter."

"Oh yes," said Mum, "she's our treasure."

"That's right," said Mr Snazzy. "Sign this form, Florence, and I shall make you and your family rich."

I looked at the fat man in a snazzy suit. We were sat in his glass office in Manchester.

"Who are you?" I asked.

"I'm Mr Snazzy, your agent."

"My agent?"

"Yes," said Mum. "Mr Snazzy is giving you a contract. He's going to manage your career."

I was puzzled. What career?

I looked at Mum and Dad, smiling. It was like I had the power to do something for them, and they were really determined I should do it.

"Do as you're told, Flo," said Dad. Your mum's set her heart on a new dishwasher and you don't want to upset her, do you?"

"SIGN," shouted Mum, excitedly. "Go on."

I looked at Mum and Dad. They seemed to be the happiest mum and dad in the world. So I picked up Mr Snazzy's golden pen and signed the form.

"POP"

Mr Snazzy poured a fizzy drink.

"Champagne!" screeched Mum.

"Fill 'em up," laughed Dad.

Mr Snazzy poured the drink into three glasses.

(I didn't get one, not even a Diet Coke!)

Tell her, Mr Snazzy" said Mum.

"Tell me what?" I asked.

"Mr Snazzy is giving you a new name."

"A new name?"

"Yes. Everyone in showbusiness has a new name," said Mr Snazzy, "and yours is…"

"HOLY FLO"

"HOLY FLO?" I said. "Why do you want to call me that?"

"Because it suits you," said Mr Snazzy. "It's your new image!"

I was confused.

"She'll get used to it," said Mum, "once the 'HOLY FLO' brand name hits the shops."

"Yes…" said Mr Snazzy, opening a golden box. "These are just the prototypes… of course… but we have here, for starters…

a HOLY FLO doll."

Mr Snazzy held up a plastic doll with long curly hair. It had a tiny weeny waist, long legs, and a gorgeous face with heart shaped lips.

"Who's that?" I asked.

"You," said Mum." Can't you tell?"

67

"But I wear glasses?"

"Not anymore…" said Mr Snazzy. "You're going to wear blue contact lenses."

"Why?"

"It's your new image!" said Mum.

"Listen to this," said Mr Snazzy, pressing a button on the doll's back.

"Geee… Life's a Miracle," said the doll.

"Cute, isn't she?" said Dad, laughing.

Mr Snazzy pressed the button again.

"I'm an angel from Heaven," said the doll.

"Oh, it's adorable," said Mum. "Better than the real thing. Erm… a pretty likeness… I mean."

"What do you think of it, Flo?" asked Dad.

"I don't speak with an American voice." I said.

"There's no pleasing you," said Mum, annoyed. "You're very moody today, aren't you?"

"The doll looks nothing like me. Why's her hair blonde and curly?"

"Because," said Mr Snazzy, "that's how your hair is going to look in your television commercial."

"My television commercial? What television commercial?"

"The television commercial you're going to make to sell all your products," said Dad.

Mr Snazzy emptied a golden box onto the table. A mountain of things fell out.

"HOLY FLO perfume!"

"HOLY FLO lipsticks!"

"HOLY FLO eye shadow!"

"HOLY FLO socks!"

"HOLY FLO… everything!"

"You're a very special lady," said Mr Snazzy.
"Am I?"
"Yes," said Dad. "Mother Mary talking with you, has made you special. That's why the public will want to buy these things. It will make them feel special, too. And you want everybody in the world to feel special, like you, don't you, Flo?"
"Oh yes, Dad." I said, "I do."
"Good," said Mum. "Then, let's get the Holy Flo goodies into the shops for Christmas."
"Yes," said Dad, "there's not a moment to lose."
"It's time to make this family rich," laughed Mr Snazzy. "It's time to make Florence Hargreaves a…

STAR!"

CHAPTER 35

Angel

"Flap your wings, honey," shouted the director. "Action."
I flapped and flapped my white, feathered wings. I flew around the film studio (on a wire), smiling at the camera. A wind machine blew my new blonde wig. And I sprayed myself with 'Holy Flo' perfume.
"You too can smell like an angel, this Christmas. Spray yourself with HOLY FLO," I said.
"Cut," said the director. "Fabulous."
"She's a born natural," said Mr Snazzy.
I did feel special dressed in a white frock, with a big pair of white feather wings on my back, and a pink flashing halo on my head. The blue contact lenses made my eyes shine ever so brightly. I felt like a fairy. But I wasn't a fairy. I was an angel.
"You look so different," said Mum. "Much better than you did."
"She's our little princess," said Dad, proudly."
I'd never had compliments like this before, ever!
"Oh, thanks, Dad," I said.
It was great having everybody's attention in the film studio. It seemed everybody liked me here. And I wanted to please them, very much.
"You're going to be the most famous little girl in the world," said Mr Snazzy.
"Really?" I said. I couldn't believe it. It was like a big dream.
"Oh yes. Without a doubt," said Mr Snazzy.
"Thanks," I said.

"When your TV commercial is shown, everybody in the world will buy your perfume."

"I hope so," I said.

"Flap your wings, honey," shouted the director (again). "Action."

I flapped and flapped my white, feathered wings. I flew around the film studio (on a wire), smiling at the camera (again). The wind machine blew my new blond wig (again), and I sprayed myself with 'Holy Flo' perfume.

"You too can smell like an angel this Christmas, Spray yourself with HOLY FLO."

"She's got what it takes," chuckled Mr Snazzy. "Holy Flo's got the magic touch."

CHAPTER 36

Knickers

Guess what?

Mr Snazzy was right.

When my TV commercial was shown, every bottle of HOLY FLO perfume began to sell fast. And my HOLY FLO doll was the gift to have that Christmas for every girl (and for a lot of boys, too). In fact, people wanted to buy everything in the 'HOLY FLO' range.

Holy Flo
bracelets,

earrings,

fridge magnets,

baseball caps,

tee shirts,

socks
and…
knickers!

People couldn't get enough of me. It was very exciting. Amazing!

'BUY INTO THE MAGIC,' said the posters.

Within a matter of weeks, my face was everywhere. It was fantastic! I was famous! Every time we peeped into a magazine, there I was - me, being an angel, selling something or other. Every time I went outside, lots of people wanted to talk with me.

"It's her!" people shouted in the street. "It's Holy Flo! The girl that talks with Holy Mary!"

Mum and Dad were so proud of me.

Mum said, "When you're a star, people want to talk with you all the time. It goes with the job."

Mum and Dad were over the moon with how everything was going (my career). They were becoming very popular themselves. The bank manager was on the phone every day, inviting Mum and Dad to his office for cake and a bottle of sherry. Mum and Dad were really chuffed.

"I've always wanted someone famous for a daughter," Mum said to Gran. "Rather than just a nobody."

I kept wondering what Mary must think about my success? But I hadn't heard from her since I'd become famous. I hoped she'd be pleased with everything. My success was never ending. For instance, that building, that Gran took me to see, the old church. Well, it had changed. It wasn't for sale anymore. And it wasn't old and musty. It had been decorated with a complete make over. When you walked inside, there were new fitted carpets, and new wooden seats with big, silk, golden cushions. There was even a drinks machine, selling bottles of 'revitalising' 'Holy Flo Water'. And there was a big photograph of me hanging on the wall (wearing a crown). "Wow!" I said, "this old church has changed. It's amazing."

"Wow, indeed," said the vicar. "A gift sent from Heaven."

CHAPTER 37

Druggies

I haven't told you about the vicar, have I? How he comes into my story? Well, I didn't have the blue rose anymore. It wasn't in the window of Gran's laundrette. Once my story was in the national newspapers, and the vicar read about it, he came round to see my gran, and asked if he could take the rose back to the church (for safe keeping). The vicar said the rose was "too precious" to be left in a jam jar, in a laundrette window. He said, "Druggies would nick it."

Gran got a bit nervous, she didn't want to be burgled, not by druggies. So we agreed the vicar should have the rose for the church and keep it safe.

"How very wise and charitable," he said.

The vicar kept the rose in a glass box. The box had a modern 'vacuum' pump. This meant a tube sucked all the air out of the glass box. It kept the rose looking alive (air tight), fresh.

The rose
couldn't
die. Ever.
It stayed fresh as a daisy! Forever (only it was a rose).

Good idea, don't you think?

CHAPTER 38

Humble

Nobody could go near the rose without the vicar's permission (not even me). "No Hands and Fingers" said a sign. So many people wanted to see the rose, the vicar decided to sell tickets. The church was full to its arches. Coach parties came from everywhere. America, Australia, China, Japan, France, Italy, Germany, Spain, Ireland (to name a few). The vicar had to remove a lot of graves to build a new car park.

"It's standing room only," said the vicar. "If this carries on, I shall have to build myself a cathedral."

The vicar was very happy. The happiest vicar in the world. He was also very humble. He thought of lots of ways to make money for charity. The vicar decided I should do some personal appearances. He invited the TV cameras along. The vicar said it was my duty to appear to as many people in the world as was humanly possible. It was called 'THE HOLY ROSE SHOW.' There was such a feeling of excitement whenever I appeared in public. I felt really good being liked a lot.

"This little girl has captured the world's imagination," said the vicar. "She is a... God-send."

"She most certainly is," said Mr Snazzy. "Her doll sales are going through the roof."

It was great. The church became so popular that the vicar decided to sell tickets for a special event. It was called,

THE CEREMONY.

CHAPTER 39

Adored

"Let the ceremony of the blue rose commence," cried the vicar. And it did. Every Sunday. This was when the vicar opened the glass box and took out the rose for everyone to see.

The church choir sang 'Happy days are here again…' and a lot of old people (some in wheelchairs, some with walking sticks), made their way towards the front of the church (to see me). I sat there watching everything on my golden throne. The vicar walked around carrying the rose on a white velvet cushion. He handed the rose to me, and I wafted the rose under the nose of every old person. Each old person gave a big sniff, and put a five pound note into the vicar's collection tin.

"Do you believe in the power of the blue rose?" asked the vicar.

"Yes! Yes!" cried the old people.

"Good!" said the vicar, "then… sniff the power of the blue rose, throw away your walking sticks and wheel away your wheelchairs. It's time to… Dance…

Let's do the hippie hippie shake."

"Oh, I can… feel the life in my old legs," shouted an old man, sniffing.

"My rheumatism has gone!" shouted an old woman, twerking.

"Dance, Dance, Dance," cried the vicar "Sniff your pain away."

It was fabulous to see. A big party atmosphere, with the vicar playing a selection of oldie music (rock and roll) on the organ, and Mrs Zandy always doing her break dancing routine (spinning on her head).

"Right on," Mrs Zandy cried. "BOOGIE WOOGIE."

It was electric (electric blue).

The old people had a brilliant time. They cheered and sniffed. And the more they sniffed the blue rose, the more they…

Danced.

Faster
and
faster,

swinging
their arms
and legs,

and
wiggling their bums!

It was a

Dance Crazy

Frenzy
Event.

The power of the blue rose. "Every Sunday at 8 o'clock"

The miracle of miracles.

Everybody kept thanking me for helping them. But I hadn't done anything. Not really. It was Mary and her blue rose that had made everything happen. I just sat on my golden throne, watching, clapping my hands, and smiling.

"Oh no. Without you, Holy Flo, seeing Mary, none of this could happen," said an old woman. "Mary has made you special. You've helped every old person in the world dance their pain away. Hallelulla!"

I didn't know what to say. I just kept smiling, and clapping my hands, like it was my birthday, and listened to all the praise. It never stopped. It was like every old person in the world I met, "liked ME."

I must admit, I did feel brilliant. I did feel…

…ADORED.

CHAPTER 40

Luxury

We moved into our luxury house in the summer. The house was built for us especially. Mum said, "I want my new house to be sparkling. It must smell fresh. I want it to be so fabulous that it makes every person that sees it, JEALOUS." And it did.

There was a garden with plastic trees, that didn't lose any leaves (and make any mess), and a lake, with a fountain, and a thousand fake goldfish (clockwork operated.) We had our tea at a long table, with a crystal chandelier above our heads, that sparkled, every night. Mum and Dad didn't have to lift a finger, no dusting or anything. A woman called Fifi came to do our cooking. She lived in a shed somewhere in the garden, and went around the house driving a big industrial hoover, removing any fluff.

Mum and Dad didn't need to worry about anything. The money from my perfume sales just kept flowing in. Dad called me "his Pot of Gold!" Mum and Dad spent hours and hours watching TV and eating chocolates.

It was a life of luxury. Truly, it was.

At the back of the luxury house, there was a room made of glass, called 'The Orangery'. It had lots of flowers, and oranges growing. This was my favourite place. I liked to sit here every morning and eat my toast. I got very friendly with a butterfly. This butterfly was called Butterfly Blue because she was a beautiful blue colour. The butterfly came to balance on my finger every day. I was glad about this, because Bert, my hamster, had died from toothache, a few months ago, before we moved. The blue butterfly was my friend. I was starting to feel a bit lonely, actually, because I didn't get to spend any time with anybody anymore. No friends. Mum and Dad were always going out to parties, and Gran lived too far away to visit. I'd just sit in the glass room and say, "I like the new house, Butterfly Blue, but when I lived in the old house, and me and George used to go to the chip shop together, and play in the park, although it wasn't a posh life, it was a nice life. It was my life, and I miss it a lot." And sometimes, when I got really honest with myself, I had to admit, I missed George, too (a lot). I hadn't seen him for a long time. I thought we'd always be friends. I thought he might have wanted to see me again, especially after I'd become rich and famous, but he hadn't tried to phone me and I hadn't phoned him. What was the point? I was too busy selling perfume and stuff. My life was different now. Dad said, "You're so valuable, Flo, we must keep you locked up."

Mum didn't like me going outside. She said I had to keep my 'Holy Flo' image nice and clean.

"Intact," she said.

I always had to wear a new white dress and a wig that always had to look long, blonde and curly.

"Pristine," said Mum.

The best way to keep my wig looking long, blond, and curly was to have seven wigs (one for each day).

"You must look immaculate." Said Mum.

So I did.

Always!

It was a bit tiring, actually.

CHAPTER 41

Ice

The only time I went outside that summer was to do my 'Holy Flo' whirlwind tour. Mr Snazzy organised everything. People paid one hundred pounds to say hello to me in big posh hotels. They got a gala dinner and a signed photo. I'd sit on my golden throne with a microphone, and I'd tell everybody in the room eating their steak and chips, about me and Mary. I'd finish off giving everyone a message, during their apple pie and custard. The message was always the same.

"Mary says she's my friend. And she's your friend also."

Everybody was pleased to hear this. It went down very well. Sometimes we had a raffle, too. This was for the poor people living in Halifax or Scunthorpe. It cheered everybody up, "helping the less fortunate". Mum always seemed to win.

"Bloomin' heck, not me again! People will start to think this raffle is fixed," cried Mum (fifty times, at least).

Everybody liked my personal appearances. Sometimes I'd visit hospitals to see the poorly people who didn't have much time left to live. I'd smile at them. It gave them a lot of hope. Their eyes would flicker and they'd try and smile back at me. Some would try and sit up.

Mum said. "They should prescribe our Flo as medicine on the National Health. She's a life saver."

"Our little saint," said Dad.

People did seem to feel a lot better after meeting me, and that made me feel I was doing some good, my new posh life did seem worth it. Even though I didn't see anyone. Even if I had no friends. Even if it felt like I was living alone most of the time, forever, inside a house of ice. I just… got on with it, I suppose.

"For the good of others," Mum said. So I did. I smiled and I waved and behaved 'immaculately'.

For everybody in the whole wide world!

CHAPTER 42

Grateful

"Millions of girls would die to have a lifestyle like yours," said Dad.

"You should be grateful," said Mum. "When I was your age, I didn't have one wig. And you've got seven!"

I did feel grateful. A lot of people wanted to live like me, I knew that. People treated me like a pop star, which was fantastic. But, I couldn't help feeling the person they were seeing wasn't really me. It was someone else. I was hidden away under my blonde wig and white dress and feathered wings. I even had to wear a crystal crown on my head, with sparkling jewels.

"A star always sparkles," said Mr Snazzy. "It goes with the job."

So, that's what I did. I sparkled for people, morning noon and night. I played the part of HOLY FLO (brilliantly). Mr Snazzy said feeling lonely was a small price to pay for making the world happy. And I suppose he was right. And whenever I was at home on my own, the blue butterfly was always flying around, waiting to see me. That was the best part, the best feeling in the world, knowing Blue was always there waiting for me. A friend. You're very lucky if you find someone to talk with when you're feeling lonely. Even an insect. Aren't you?

CHAPTER 43

Annoyed

"Right then, we're off," said Mum. "Don't answer the door while we're away, strangers might nick something."

Mum and Dad had twenty five big suitcases with them.

"Where you going?" I asked.

"We're going on a world cruise," squealed Mum, excited.

"Surprise Surprise" said Dad. "We'll be gone away for six months."

"Six months?" I said, shocked. "That's a long time."

"Well, it's a very big world," said Mum, "with lots to see."

"Can't I come?"

"No. You can't." said Dad.

"Why not?"

"Contractual obligations," said Mum

"What does that mean?"

"It means," said Mum, "you've got to stay here and work."

"But… I'll feel more lonely," I said.

"Then talk to Mary," said Dad.

"I've tried," I said, "but Mary is still away talking with the Blue Buddha, I think."

"Then try harder," said Dad. "Our cruise is booked."

"Oh," I said, feeling really fed up. "Well… have a nice time" (without me).

"We will," said Mum. "We're sailing first class with all the trimmings. Bon voyage, Flo."

"Ta ra," said Dad (without kissing me goodbye).

After they'd gone, I was sad. I cried for a bit, and then I got a bit annoyed, because I thought, why should I stop here and work, while Mum and Dad sail away on a world cruise? But Gran said, "Never mind. You don't have to go around the world to have an adventure. Me and you can still enjoy ourselves together, can't we, like old times?"

"Yes," I said.

I was pleased Gran was looking after me now, in the new house. It would be like old times, when I got to see Gran every day.

Gran gave Fifi (the maid) 'leave of absence'. That meant she got off work every day, with full pay. Gran said, "I can do all the household duties myself, thank you."

Gran brought her own mop and bucket. It was great.

CHAPTER 44

Crazy

"What shall we do today, Flo?"

"I don't know," I said.

"I'll tell you what," said Gran, "Shall I make you some chips, fried in the chip shop way?"

"Oh yes," I said. "It would make a change from eating Mum's luxury caviar."

"Righto," said Gran, "chips it is. Fried in the old style, and made from real potatoes."

"Awesome," I said.

Gran peeled some potatoes and fried them in a big pan. Then, we sat down together and had a great big feast, eating chip butties with loads of tomato sauce. It was perfect (like old times). After this, we decided I should answer my fan mail. If it's left too long, it builds up and you can't open the front door. I get sack loads (millions and millions). Most of the letters are from people asking for miracles.

"There's a man writing here," said Gran, "from America, who wants to know if Mary can help him lose some weight, for his honeymoon."

"What should I say, Gran?"

"Let's write and tell him to cut out the steak and kidney pies."

"Good idea," I said, "and donuts."

Me and Gran really enjoyed answering the fan letters. It made us both feel useful.

"Oh, would you look at this one," said Gran. "This is a posh letter. It must be from a very important person, indeed."

"Who?" I said.

Gran opened the letter carefully. "Oh, it's from The Prime Minister," she gasped. "He wants you to go and see him in London. He says he's got a big surprise. He's heard all about you, Flo. He calls you a 'phenomenon!'"

"What's does that mean?" I asked.

Gran was puzzled.

"I'm not sure, love."

I looked at the Prime Minister's letter. It was typed, with no spelling mistakes.

"Look," I said, "the letter says I can take a guest."

"Oh, I've never been to London," said Gran, clapping her hands with excitement.

"Shall we go together?" I said. "And see what the Prime Minster wants. His big surprise?"

"Good idea." squealed Gran. "How exciting."

Crazy or what?

CHAPTER 45

Surprise

The Prime Minister's office smelt of polish and disinfectant. Everything looked neat and tidy. There wasn't one fly buzzing anywhere, not even a bluebottle hiding behind the net curtains (Gran had a look). I could smell the Prime Minister's aftershave. It smelt like turnips and radishes.

About fifty people waited for us, in the 'Media Room', some holding cameras, and others holding microphones.

"Sit down next to me," whispered the Prime Minister.

Gran and me sat down with the Prime Minister and faced the room of people. The Prime Minister took hold of a microphone.

"Ladies and gentlemen," he said, "I've invited you here today, in honour of this very special little lady. I've been a great fan, ever since I read Holy Flo's story. She is a great role model for young people, and is very much loved by the elderly, ever since she helped rid them of their pains and got them dancing again with the aid of her blue rose. And, it gives me great pleasure, on behalf of my government, to hand over to Holy Flo this very special award, in recognition of her success."

The Prime Minister handed me a glass bowl with my name engraved on it. I looked at it. Gran looked at it. It looked like a fruit bowl.

I was puzzled.

"What's this?" I asked.

"It's your big surprise," said the Prime Minister proudly. "For services to Britain."

"Come again?" said Gran.

"My government has named Holy Flo, Businesswoman of the Year."

I didn't know what to say. I looked at Gran and she looked at me. And we both looked at the fruit bowl.

"But... I'm not a woman," I said.

"Not yet," said the Prime Minister, "but you will be, one day. Smile for the media, Florence. Let them take our photograph together."

The Prime Minister shook my hand. He wouldn't let go, he held my hand very tight. Photographers started taking our photo. I was nearly blinded by the flashbulbs.

"Tell the media what you think of me," whispered the Prime Minister. "Let them know I'm your... friend."

The Prime Minister smiled, so close, his teeth looked frightening, like massive plastic tombstones. I said nothing. He wasn't my friend. We'd only just met.

"This little girl has achieved a great deal," continued the Prime Minister." "The Holy Flo brand is selling faster than tea cakes. She's bringing a great deal of money into the country and I'm very pleased indeed."

"What does all this mean?" I whispered to Gran.

"It means you're a phenomenon."

"Really?" I said.

"Oh yes," said the Prime Minister. "My government always likes a success story, especially during an election year." The Prime Minister put his hand over the microphone. "I don't suppose your friend Mary has a message for me?" he whispered. "If she does, now would be a good time to mention it, don't you think?"

"What kind of message?" I asked.

"Well," said the Prime Minister, "Does Mary give me her blessing? Is she my friend? Does she think the British people should vote for me in the upcoming election?"

"I don't know," I said.

"Well ask her, silly," said the Prime Minister. He sounded a bit annoyed (like we were both playing a game and I wasn't playing it properly). It was then I heard something, clear as a whistle.

A voice.
In my head.
It was her.

Mary.

She was here!

CHAPTER 46

Message

"Oh I can hear something," I said.

"What can you hear?" said the Prime Minister, hopefully.

"Mary. She's talking to me, inside my head. She's got a message for you."

"Really?" said the Prime Minister, clapping his hands together. "How marvellous. What does Mary have to say?"

The Prime Minister pushed the microphone into my face. The media seemed very excited. They waited for my answer. There was a great big hush.

"Mary wants you to go to the bank," I said.

"And take out a load of money."

"Really?" said the Prime Minister, "Why?"

"She wants you to give it away."

"What?" said the Prime Minister, shocked. "Give away money?"

"Yes."

"Who to?"

"Tramps."

"Tramps?" cried the Prime Minister.

"Yes," I said.

"What on earth for?"

"So they can buy something nice to eat, like… KitKats?"

"KitKats?" shouted the prime minister. His face went red, like a beetroot. For some reason, he didn't seem very pleased. "Is that Mary's only message?"

"I think so," I said.

I listened if Mary had got anything more to say, but she hadn't. She'd gone. The Prime Minister didn't look very happy. He stood up.

"Will you excuse me?" he said.

The media started talking at once. They went bonkers. They wanted to know what the Prime Minister thought of Mary's message. They stopped him leaving the room.

"Do you intend giving money away to tramps?" a journalist shouted.

"No comment," said the Prime Minister.

"What about KitKats? Do you think tramps should be able to buy KitKats?"

"Of course not," said The Prime Minister, annoyed.

"Why not?" asked another journalist.

The Prime Minister stood with his mouth open like he was thinking what to say but no words came out. He quickly darted away, leaving me and Gran. Everybody could hear the Prime Minister shouting in the next room. He was in a terrible mood. Me and Gran didn't know what to do. It was embarrassing.

"Get that little brat and old bag out of here!" cried the Prime Minister. "Meeting them both has been a fiasco! Everything has backfired! Holy Flo didn't tell everyone I was her friend, and neither did Mary. They are no help to me winning this year's election. All this talk of tramps and giving money away for KitKats is ridiculous."

"I don't think the Prime Minister is pleased with you," whispered Gran, "or with Mary's message."

"Or with KitKats," I laughed.

"Does Mary like tramps?" asked a journalist.

"Mary likes everybody," I said.

"Including the Prime Minister?" asked another journalist.

"No comment," said Gran. "Come on, Flo, let's get going. Before they throw us out. Where's my handbag?"

I don't think Gran was too impressed with meeting the Prime Minister. And neither was I. We didn't like his fruit bowl either (it was made of plastic). We found Gran's handbag and quickly left the Prime minister's house. It was a big let-down, really. The Prime Minster wasn't a friendly man. He was an angry man. Me and Gran were glad to get outside, for some fresh air, and buy a hot dog.

CHAPTER 47

Castle

Gran suggested we make the best of our trip to London and not let the Prime minister spoil it. We got a taxi and decided to see the London sights. Gran was thrilled to bits. We saw Trafalgar square, Tower bridge, the Tower of London, Big Ben, and the River Thames. It was a whirlwind tour.

"Oh, it's a big place, isn't it?" said Gran, looking through the taxi window. "Lots of people rushing everywhere. It's too fast for me." Gran wanted to see where the Queen lived. She liked Queen Mavis. Gran and the Queen had grown up at the same time only in different places. They were the same age. They shared the same birthday, but had never shared the same birthday cake. We decided to stop the taxi at the Queen's Castle and get out. We bought ourselves an ice cream. Lots of tourists were doing the same. Everybody seemed excited. Gran and me wondered if the Queen's castle had one window cleaner or two?

"It must take ages," said Gran. "No sooner than you'd finished cleaning the last window, you'd have to start cleaning the first window again."

The Queen's castle had one hundred windows, at least. It was very interesting seeing where the Queen lived. She didn't have any chipped paint around her windows or any rubbish in her front yard, just lots of horse poo.

"Manure," said Gran.

We had a good time. We were just about to leave, when suddenly a tourist started shouting and pointing up at a castle window.

"Look, look."

We all looked up to see a woman, wearing a velvet frock, white, long gloves, and hair curlers. She was holding a pair of golden binoculars and looking into the crowd. Then, another tourist started shouting,

"It's the Queen! Queen Mavis. She's looking at someone."

"Who?" asked Gran.

"You!" cried the tourist. "The Queen is looking at you."

Then all the tourists started looking at me and shouting,

"It's her! It's her! It's Holy Flo!"

"I told you to wear your dark sunglasses, and an old tatty wig," said Gran. "You've been recognised."

The tourists were very pleased to see me. They wanted my autograph. They forget all about the Queen.

"We love you, Holy Flo," said the tourists.

"We buy all your perfumes and everything."

I began to sign autographs and smile for their selfies. I looked up to see if the Queen was annoyed at me, getting all the attention. I was surprised to see the Queen waving, at me.

What did she want?

Then, I felt someone tap me on my shoulder, and when I turned round it was one of the Queen's guards (the ones who wear red coats and big, shiny black boots).

"Her Majesty The Queen wants to meet Holy Flo," said the guard.

"Why? I said, amazed.

"She's a fan!"

"Bloomin' heck," said Gran. "What a royal turn up!"

CHAPTER 48

Feet

Me and Gran were very nervous. We couldn't believe it, both of us sitting with Queen Mavis inside her castle and having tea. The Queen's parlour was very posh, with big old paintings, a plush flowered carpet, stuffed animals, pretty table lamps, bowls of Bombay Mix, and very old mirrors.

"Do have a scone," said the Queen, graciously.

"Thank you," I said

"Will you butter one yourself, or shall I ring for a servant to do it?"

"We'll do it ourselves," said Gran. "We don't want to cause any fuss."

"Very well. Eat as many scones as you like," said the Queen. I usually feed what's left to Winnie, Madge and Violet, but not today."

"Who's Winnie, Madge and Violet?" I asked.

"The royal poodles," said the Queen, pointing underneath her sofa with a lacy serviette. Three white poodles, wearing diamond collars, lay watching (in a bad mood).

"They're on a diet," said the Queen, "before our hols. I'm afraid they'll never climb up all those Whitby winding cobbled streets if they don't lose some weight. They'll be too puffed out."

"Do poodles eat scones?" asked Gran.

"Mine eat anything." said the Queen. "Even marzipan and sprouts."

Her Majesty buttered herself a scone, graciously, and took a delicate bite.

"What brings you to London, pray?"

"The Prime Minister invited me," I said. "He's made me Businesswoman Of The Year. He gave me a plastic fruit bowl."

"The old Tom cat," said the Queen, unimpressed.

I don't think the Queen liked the Prime Minister very much.

"Lovely scones," said Gran.

"Aren't they?" said the Queen. "Tesco's Finest."

Gran was surprised by this.

"I would have thought you'd have shopped at Marks and Spencer's," said Gran. "You being the Queen."

"I used to," said the Queen. "But ever since the Prime Minister started poking his nose into my financial affairs, I've had to buy my scones elsewhere. It's the cutbacks. The Prime Minister's a very mean man. He's making royal life very difficult for me. A misery."

"I'm sure," said Gran. "You can't be a Queen and live on the cheap."

"Quite," sighed Her Majesty. "Being a Queen requires a certain royal lifestyle, and that costs money. For instance, these white cotton gloves I'm wearing are worn out already, and I only bought them a month ago. It's all the royal waveabouts. I'm a very busy Queen, shaking many hands and so forth."

"I'm sure." said Gran. "On your feet all day."

"Oh yes," groaned the Queen. "Heavens. Oh, don't remind me."

I noticed the Queen started rubbing one of her feet (although she tried to hide it).

"And how is Mary, nowadays," asked the Queen (changing the subject).

"Good." I said. "She's been away, visiting the Blue Buddha."

"How lovely," said the Queen.

Again, I noticed the Queen rubbing one of her feet. Although this time, Her Majesty rubbed the other foot. "Ouch," she winced.

The Queen seemed to be in some discomfort. But I didn't say anything. When you're in the presence of a Queen, you have to watch your manners. But something was troubling Her Majesty, I could tell. What could it be?

CHAPTER 49

Pain

The Queen sipped her tea. "I've heard about the blue rose," she said. "I think it wonderful. Simply Divine. A very special gift."

"Yes," I said. "The rose has helped so many old people with their aches and pains and got them dancing again."

The Queen looked at me. It seemed she wanted to ask me something, but was afraid to say. She was fidgeting on her royal throne.

"Is anything the matter, Your Majesty?" asked Gran.

"I don't know if I dare tell you?" said the Queen.

"Tell us what?" I said.

"Well," said the Queen, "I, myself, have been in a lot of pain recently, and nobody has been able to help me. I've been to see the best doctors in the land, but… alas, they tell me nothing can be done. The doctors call it a mild discomfort, but it's not. Oh, the pain is excruciating."

"Really?" I said.

"Yes," said the Queen. "Perhaps if I were to slip off my royal footwear and show you my feet, all will be explained? Do you mind?"

"We don't mind, do we, Gran?"

"Oh, no," said Gran. "Feel free, Your Majesty. We're all friends here. We have no problems with your royal feet being on show."

"I'm afraid my royal feet are not a pretty sight," said the Queen, slipping off her royal shoes. She was embarrassed. The Queen suffered (one on each foot) from knobbly lumps around her big toes. It was a shame. Not pretty.

"I've made excuses for years," sighed the Queen. "Every time I have a royal dinner party and the band starts playing oom pah pah, there's always someone who asks me to dance, but I'm afraid I always have to decline. I have two bunions you see. One on each royal foot. My bunions are too painful for dancing."

"I see," said Gran, shocked.

The Queen wiggled both her feet and sighed. The bunions were purple and pink (both throbbing). They looked like bruised mushrooms!

"Oh, can you help me, Holy Flo?" pleaded The Queen. "Oh, do say you can help my royal feet."

It was terrible to see the Queen suffering with her bunions. I knew I had to do something. So I said, "Might I make a phone call your Majesty and talk it over with someone in the know? An expert."

"Of course," said the Queen. "Anything, if it will help. The royal bunions are in your healing hands, Holy Flo."

Oh, what a responsibility!

"Very well," I said, "leave your royal feet to me."

CHAPTER 50

Secret

I told the vicar about the Queen's bunions, on the phone. The vicar arrived, quickly. "Do not worry, Your Majesty," he said, "we'll have your royal tootsies back to normality in no time."

The vicar had flown to the palace by royal helicopter. He said he'd be honoured to help with the Queen's bunion problem.

"It's my privilege and duty as a servant to the crown, ma'am."

The Queen was very pleased.

"I'm so grateful to you, Vicar. I would have come to see you in your church, but I do find my bunions ever so embarrassing. I like to keep them a secret."

"Don't be embarrassed, Your Majesty," said the vicar. "I believe bunions are very common in a woman of your age."

"Yes," said the Queen, "but I'm a Queen, and a Queen can't afford to be seen as common, can she?"

"You've got a point there," said Gran.

"Your secret is safe with me," said the vicar. "Do not fear, I shall tell nobody."

"Oh goodie," said the Queen. "Now, to business. What happens next? What should I do?"

"Do?" said the vicar.

"What is the procedure? Do I have to lie down on my velvet chaise longue or anything?"

"No," said the vicar, pulling on a pair of rubber gloves.

"Might it be better if I removed my tights?" asked the Queen, rather shyly.

"Whatever for?" said the vicar, shocked.

"Well… to let the air circulate, let my feet breath freely."

"No," said the vicar, "that won't be necessary. The blue rose will work its power through your tights. The magic is very strong. It can even work through a pair of trousers."

"Very well," said the Queen (she was very impressed, I could tell). "Let us begin."

"I need you to stand here with me," said the vicar, "while Flo waves the rose under your nose, like so."

"Then… what?" asked the Queen.

"You sniff it," I said.

"I inhale the rose?" said the Queen.

"Yes," I said, "deep breaths."

"Is that all that's required?" asked the Queen.

"Yes," I said. "Give the rose a big sniff and its beautiful perfume will do the rest."

"Very well," said the Queen, standing in the middle of her royal parlour. "Let the ceremony of the blue rose commence."

CHAPTER 51

Pong

The vicar opened the glass box, and took out the blue rose very gently (not wanting any of the petals to fall). He held the rose in his rubber gloved hands and gave the rose to me. I pointed the rose into the Queen's face. The Queen took her glasses off and got ready to sniff. You could tell she meant business. Her nose was twitching like a horse.

"Inhale the perfume of the rose," said the vicar. "May the pain of your royal bunions vanish and your dancing days commence again."

Queen Mavis closed her eyes,
in deep concentration,
she sniffed.

"Oooooooooooh," she said. "The rose smells like fresh raindrops with a hint of morning sunshine." We all waited to see what would happen next. Even the Queen's poodles came out from underneath the sofa and sat watching, but…

nothing
happened.

"How do your bunions feel now, Your Majesty?" asked Gran.
"They feel… just the same," sighed the Queen, "painful… and throbbing."

"Oh dear," said Gran.

The vicar grabbed the rose out of my hands and wafted the rose into the Queen's face with more strength. "Sniff again," said the vicar, "let the power of the blue rose fill you up with exultation."

"I'm trying," said the Queen.

Her Majesty took a bigger sniff. The vicar wafted the rose even faster (only this time, he did it more like he was waving a magic wand around a pumpkin).

"Sniff it… Sniff it…" cried the vicar. "Feel the pong."

The Queen sniffed and sniffed. We waited and waited, hoping the rose would do it's magic. The Queen's poodles didn't move. They watched everything, very still, like they were made of stone. Three statues.

But…
again,
nothing
happened.

It was very disappointing.

Then…
"Oh."
suddenly,
the Queen…
…started
…swaying
and…

"Oooooooooooh," she moaned, "I'm feeling… something… oooooooooooh… something is… happening!"

CHAPTER 52

Wobble

The Queen began to wobble, all over!

"That's more like it," shouted the vicar. "Go with it, Your Majesty, don't fight it. SNIFF."

The Queen did it again.

A huge sniiiiiiiiiiiiiiiiiiiiif.

She went with it.

Sniiiiiiiiiiiiiiiiiif. Sniffffffffffffffffffff. PONG.

Then
the Queen
began to wobble and tremble,
more and more
(violently).

"Ooooooooooooooooooooooooooooooooooooooooooooooooh," she groaned.

"You're getting the pong of it now," shouted the vicar. "It's coming at you like ocean waves mixed with furious lightning."

The Queen's eyelids began to flicker and her eyelashes began to flutter. Suddenly, the Queen started to tremble and wobble like a big enormous jellyfish.

"Ooooooooooooh," she cried, "my big toes are twitching."

And they were.

Her Majesty's big toes were twitching, like fat tadpoles.

"How's your royal bunions now?" cried the vicar.

"Good gracious," cried the Queen, "both my bunions… feel… as light… as Parisian soufflés!

"Ohhhhhhhhhhhhhhhhhhhhhhhhhhhhhhhhhhhhhhhhhhh,
my royal feet… feel… all of a sudden… very floaty floaty!
Ohhhhhhhhhhhhhhhhhhhhhhhhhhhhhhhhhhhhhhhhhhh,
my royal legs feel like… prancing… and… dancing… My bunions have lost all sense of pain! I am in ecstasy!"

Suddenly, the Queen started dancing, twirling and twirling around the room.

"Weeeeeeeeeeeeee!" she screamed. "Weeeeeeeeeeeeee!"

CHAPTER 53

Cha Cha

The Queen cocked her leg into the air and jumped over her throne. The poodles started barking (one of them attacked a cushion) with excitement. The Queen began to dance. She danced and danced and danced.

"What dance is the Queen doing?" I said. "That's not the hippie hippie shake?"

"No," said the Queen, "it's the cha cha. Come on Winnie, Madge, and Violet, dance with Mummy."

The Queen's poodles ran across the carpet and started to prance around the Queen's feet. The Queen and her poodles danced everywhere, "one two three, cha cha…" They danced all over the royal carpets.

"It's magic!" cried the Queen. "I feel like I could cha cha forever."

The poodles wouldn't stop barking. They were very pleased to see Her Majesty dancing again. Me and Gran clapped our hands together with happiness and the vicar danced with the rose in his mouth. It was a very joyful moment. We were very pleased for the Queen to be free of her bunion pain. The Queen quickly jumped over a velvet pouffe. And twirled and twirled, spinning.

"At last! My big toes are free" cried the Queen "How can I ever repay you?"

"Shall we call it a thousand pounds?" said the vicar. "A donation to the Church Club funds would be very much appreciated."

"Yes. Of course," said the Queen. "I'll fetch my purse. It's in my royal handbag."

I looked at Gran and she looked at me.

"I don't think we should charge the Queen for her bunion miracle" I whispered.

"No," whispered Gran. "Of course we shouldn't."

"Why not?" whispered the vicar "It's my duty to look after the Parish. This money will come in very useful for a security camera on my South Side porch."

"A thousand pounds, it is," said the Queen, counting out her money, in crisp clean brand new notes. "And cheap at twice the price!" She laughed. "Oh, I'm so royally thrilled. Thank you."

"Thank you," said the vicar, taking the money. "Your bunion secret is safe with me."

Gran and me watched the vicar sticking the money into his fat wallet. We were not very pleased with him charging the Queen a thousand pounds (or snatching the rose out of my hand). We were very annoyed with him. But Queen Mavis didn't seem bothered. She just kept on dancing.

"One, two, three, cha cha," she cried. "My feet feel like a young pretty girl's. Oh, I'm like a brand new dancing princess!"

CHAPTER 54

News

"Who's told them?" I said, shocked.

"Well, I didn't tell them," said Gran, "and you didn't tell them, and I'm sure the Queen didn't tell them, so it must have been…"

"The vicar!" I cried. "The vicar's told the Daily Rag newspaper about the Queen's secret."

"Yes," said Gran.

"He's acting like the Queen himself," I said. "Giving out royal news."

Gran and me were eating toast in the new house. We were still mad about the vicar charging the Queen a thousand pounds for a sniff of the rose. And now this! Telling the Daily Rag about the Queen's feet.

"ROSE CURES QUEEN'S BUNIONS"

"It's outrageous," cried Gran. "Have you spoken to Mary about it?"

"No," I said, "not yet."

This wasn't the truth. I had tried talking it over with Mary. But I hadn't heard much from her recently. I couldn't get her to come and see me. Not in my head or anywhere. There seemed to be some mental blockage. I was beginning to think something was wrong? Perhaps I should never have let the vicar look after the rose? I should have been more careful. After all, Mary gave the rose to me. Not the vicar. It was my gift.

"You're too easily swayed, sometimes," said Gran. "Pushy people always take advantage of you."

"Do you think?"

"Yes." said Gran.

I was beginning to think Gran might be right. I did do a lot of things nowadays just to please people (like Mum, Dad, and Mr Snazzy).

"Do you think I should do something about it?" I said.

"Yes," said Gran.

"Like what?"

"Get the rose back."

"Oh yes," I said. "What a good idea. I'll get the rose back from the vicar today. And that will show him I'm no pushover."

"Good girl" said Gran. "That will show people you're strong."

I was just putting on my coat to go and see the vicar, when we heard a loud noise outside.

"What's that row?" said Gran.

I opened the front door, and was amazed to see a hundred people standing outside, shouting. It was a mob, jeering and waving their fists. Mum and Dad were climbing out of a taxi and trying to make their way up the garden path.

"Get out of my way," shouted Mum. "I'm not in the mood."

"What are you doing back here?" I called. "I thought you'd gone on a world cruise?"

"It's been cancelled," shouted Dad,"

"Why?"

"Food poisoning," cried Mum. "We only got as far as the Coconut Isles and the ship turned around."

"Mice droppings in the cheesecake," said Dad. "We've been sat on the toilet for three weeks. Dicky tummies."

The jeering mob didn't seem to care. They started booing Mum and Dad.

"What are all these unfriendly people doing, standing in my garden?" asked Mum.

I've no idea" I said.

"Boo, Boo," jeered the mob.

Mum and Dad tried to ignore them, but the jeering mob wouldn't let Mum and Dad into the house. They kept waving their fists and shouting more and more.

"Boo, Boo, Boo."

"Go away." shouted Mum.

But the jeering mob wouldn't.

"If you don't clear off," cried Dad, "I'll get my hosepipe out."

"You're a fake!," shouted a man.

"Who's a fake?" said Mum.

"She's a fake," shouted a woman, pointing at me. The jeering mob started to hit Mum and Dad on the head with rolled up newspapers. Things were really turning nasty.

"Oh, this is getting out of hand," said Gran.

I was shocked.

Mum and Dad were gobsmacked.

"What do all these people want, Flo?" screamed Mum (she was losing it).

"Holy Flo has been found out," shouted a woman, holding up the Daily Gossip.

I couldn't believe the newspaper's headline.

"HOLY FLO LIES" it said. "BIG TIME!"

What the heck did that mean?

CHAPTER 55

Nozzle

Two hours later, Mum and Dad finally got into the house (with the help of the fire brigade). We quickly bolted the front door. Gran made Mum and Dad a pot of tea and switched on the TV (to drown the mob's jeering outside).

Oh my goodness!

Guess what?

You'll never guess who we saw on TV? It was Julie, from school. Julie was on the Gloria Riccardo show!

What was she up to?

Well! I soon found out.

She was giving an 'exclusive interview!'

"It's a fake," said Julie."
"What is?" asked Gloria.
"The blue rose." said Julie. "And if the blue rose is a fake," said Julie, "then it stands to reason, Flo Hargreaves is a fake, too."
"Yes it does," hissed Miss Tickle, my ex schoolteacher (sat next to Julie). Miss Tickle was wearing a low cut blouse and showing off her busts.

"Who are you?" said Gloria.

"I'm Miss Tickle, Julie's schoolteacher, and I've come here today to give Julie support. I was Flo Hargreaves' teacher, until she got kicked out of school. I knew she was a liar. I always thought she was fake."

I thought to myself, you've got room to talk. It was obvious that Miss Tickle wasn't on TV to give Julie support, she was there to push herself into the media spotlight. Miss Tickle always wanted to be famous and marry a footballer. She hated teaching. She only did it to pay for hair extensions. We all knew that. Everybody said so in the school playground.

"What makes you think Holy Flo is a fake?" asked Gloria. "Where is your evidence?"

Julie couldn't wait to tell Gloria Riccardo everything, her story, you could tell. Julie smiled into the television camera.

"Well… my Aunty Ethel is a cleaner at the church. She goes there every day and hoovers the carpets."

"Yes, I do," said a tiny old lady, sat next to Julie.

"Aunty Ethel has… confessed to everything," said Julie.

"Confessed?" said Gloria."

"Yes," said Julie, "the day Flo Hargreaves gave the rose to the vicar, to keep it safe in his church, was the day my Aunty Ethel had an accident."

"Accident?" said Gloria.

"Yes," said Julie, smiling. "It was my Aunty Ethel's job to hoover the altar and keep it clean. Aunty Ethel was very jittery about going near the blue rose because it was priceless. She was supposed to hoover inside the glass box, carefully. And remove any dust or greenflies from the petals."

"That's true," said Aunty Ethel.

"But..." continued Julie, "while she was hoovering... Aunty Ethel's hand slipped and she SUCKED the rose up her nozzle."

"Her nozzle?" cried Gloria, mortified.

"Yes," said Aunty Ethel, quivering. "I sucked Mary's blue rose up the nozzle of my hoover!"

CHAPTER 56

Substitute

A hoover!

I couldn't believe what I was hearing. Neither could Mum, Dad and Gran. We were shocked. Big time.

"The rose was sucked up the nozzle of Aunty Ethel's hoover?" said Gloria, amazed.
"Yes!" wailed Aunty Ethel, "I was in such a panic. I quickly switched off the hoover, and emptied the hoover bag. But there wasn't any rose left, just a load of shrivelled blue petals."
"No!" cried Gloria.
"Yes," said Julie. "Aunty Ethel didn't tell anyone. She was frightened she'd get into trouble. So… she quickly went into the graveyard and found another rose.

A white rose.

She nicked it from a gravestone, and went home and painted the white rose…

Blue."

"No!" cried Gloria.
"Yes," said Julie. "Aunty Ethel replaced Mary's rose with a substitute."

"A substitute?" cried Gloria (nearly fainting).

"Yes," said Miss Tickle, smiling.

"But… if it wasn't Mary's rose the old people sniffed in church, whose rose was it?" cried Gloria.

"A dead man's," cried Aunty Ethel. "From Wigan!"

"Oh," said Gloria. "And… if it wasn't Mary's rose, how could it make Her Majesty the Queen's pains go away? How could it make the old people dance again?"

"Because," said Julie, "Flo Hargreaves can make people believe what she wants them to believe. Look how 'charmingly' she flogs her ponging perfume on the telly. People will believe anything she tells them. Butter wouldn't melt in her mouth. All she cares about is money. She's a big story teller. She was thrown out of school for it. LYING."

"Shiver me timbers!" cried Gloria. "This is a deadly serious business! If Florence Hargreaves can convince the Queen she is sniffing something magical, to help her bunions, then nobody in the world is safe. Not even the President of America. Or His Pontiff the Pope. Holy Flo must be stopped! She's… a born… lethal…

…liar!"

CHAPTER 57

Burst

"Rubbish," said Gran, turning off the TV in disgust. "I won't listen to this nonsense anymore. Even if the rose was replaced by Aunty Ethel, it doesn't explain why Mrs Zandy started dancing the hippie hippie shake in my laundrette. She sniffed the blue rose before the vicar got his hands on it, and before it went up the nozzle of any hoover. I saw Mrs Zandy with my own eyes, do it, and nobody can tell me I didn't. And that's the truth."

Suddenly, a helicopter appeared, flying over the house and a bunch of journalists started shouting from the open window of their cockpit with a megaphone.

"Come out, come out and explain yourself, Florence Hargreaves. Are you a liar or not?"

When I heard them shouting, I thought, enough is enough. I've had enough of all this rubbish, everybody pushing me around and accusing me of things. I thought of what Gran had said earlier, about finding the strength to stand up for myself. Be myself. So I flung open the window and shouted up at the helicopter, "Get lost! Go away! I know nothing about Mary's rose being a fake. It wasn't my fault. I'm not a fake! I'm not a LIAR! I'm Florence Hargreaves, a girl that's fed up. Big time.

And

that's…

The Truth."

I slammed down the window and started to scream. Mum covered her face with a cushion, and started rolling about on the sofa. She couldn't cope. Dad started punching the living room wall with his fists, in anger. I was fuming. I wanted to burst the world apart. I wanted to crack into tiny pieces, I was so mad.

"Oh, don't upset yourself," said Gran, trying to comfort me. "This story of Julie and Aunty Ethel will go away, you'll see. And once people understand that you knew nothing about the blue rose being replaced or being sucked up the nozzle of a hoover, they'll see you're not to blame for anything. You've done nothing wrong, Flo."

Gran was very sure of this. She believed every story should end happily. I crossed my fingers, and hoped Gran was right, with all my heart. I blew my nose and cried myself to sleep. Tomorrow would be different, I hoped. A different story, with a happy ending. But…

CHAPTER 58

Shocking

Gran got it wrong.
My story didn't have a happy ending…
It got worse.

And Worse.

The story of Mary's fake rose was told in every newspaper and on every news programme. It went on Twitter and Facebook. Everywhere. And nobody was happy with me. People said I was "a manipulating, calculating little liar." They said I'd made up the story of Mary and the blue rose, because I wanted to be rich and famous. They said I was rubbish! And I worshipped… money.
I had to stay in my bedroom and hide. My life wasn't safe, so many people wanted to get their hands on me. They said I should be locked up for at least fifty years and nobody should talk to me ever again. I was so upset. Really, really upset. Then, just when I thought things couldn't get any worse, something more awful and shocking happened… Oh dear!

…When the old people read in the newspapers the rose hadn't been Mary's (it was a replacement), they stopped dancing. Their pains came back. They fell down in supermarkets, post offices, and pubs, and some of them cracked their hips, and some split their heads open and some had to wear bandages. The hospitals were full. Nobody could get into A&E. There were queues everywhere, and the doctors and nurses were so overworked, they went on strike, and the Prime Minister went berserk, and none of the old people could dance again. They went back to being old and doddery. Their dancing days were over. They found themselves sitting down in their wheelchairs, and hobbling around with walking sticks. Even the Queen stopped dancing the cha cha. Her bunions were painful. "Throbbing." "Most royally." "Big Time."

And then, the old peoples' families went to see their solicitors and every one of them started to complain about me!

"For making the old people of the world believe in something that wasn't true."

"She's a con woman," said Mrs Zandy in the Daily Rag. "A lying toad. I shall never forgive her."

"We want compensation," the old people cried. "We shall sue! We shall sue!"

CHAPTER 59

Bonfires

Mum and Dad went into meltdown. They didn't know what to do. They told everybody I was suffering from a breakdown, brought on by spots.

"She's only a child," said Mum. "It's not our Flo's fault. Mr Snazzy's the one to blame. He put the ideas about selling perfume and everything into her mind. He should be locked up."

Unfortunately, Mum shouldn't have reminded people about my perfume, because as soon as it was mentioned, it made people think they had bought into something that wasn't Magical.

"It's just a load of rubbish," said The Daily Rag.
"Water, mixed with mint and lemons."
And then, all the people in the world started sending their bottles of perfume back to the shops saying,
"It stinks."
All the people in the world started making bonfires of the Holy Flo merchandise. Caps, fridge magnets, knickers, everything!

They burnt the lot!

Everybody in the world wanted their money back. Everybody in the world started to shout, "We'll sue. We'll sue!" I couldn't believe what was happening. My life had turned into a huge enormous nightmare. I wasn't known to the general public as Holy Flo anymore, I was known as

'THAT HORRIBLE GIRL WHO LIED TO THE QUEEN AND SOLD RUBBISH ON THE TELLY'

"Let's try and look on the bright side," said Gran.
"I'm sure there must be some good going to come out of this story. I'm sure things can only get better?

But they didn't. Things didn't get better. OH NO! They got worse.
A lot lot lot worse.
Because…
a load of policemen with walkie-talkies and barking killer dogs, knocked down our front door in the early hours of Sunday morning. And… they arrested Mum and Dad!
"Lock 'em up," shouted a woman, walking her terrier.
"Throw away the key," shouted a man, walking his rabbit.
"Oh, look what you've done to us, FLORENCE! screamed Mum.
"It's a nightmare!" shouted Dad.
"Worse than any nightmare!" shouted Mum.
And it was, because nobody could wake up from it. Our lives were turning into…

…hell!

CHAPTER 60

Safe

"You're both on trial for conning the public out of money," said the judge.

"We didn't do anything wrong, Your Honour," sobbed Mum. "If I'm guilty of anything, it's only because I wanted a nice life with a new sofa."

"We're innocent, Your Worship," pleaded Dad.

"Let the jury be the judge of that," said the Judge.

Oh, it was terrible. And there was nothing I could do.

While Mum and Dad were in court, me and Gran were at home, reading about everything in the newspaper. I felt so worried, everything was driving me daft. I decided to go on a bus ride by myself. I needed to get away. I didn't care where the bus was going, to the other end of the universe would be good! I don't know how it happened, but I ended up getting off the bus outside the church. I found myself walking through the wooden doors and up to the painting of Mary and looking into her eyes. I found myself saying, "I'm really angry. I'm fuming. I'm really mad."

"Mad about what?"

I turned around and there she was. Mary, sat on a wooden chair, alone.

"This… Holy Flo business," I said. "It's got out of hand."

"Yes," said Mary. "Whenever I appear in public, there is usually a bit of a fuss."

"A bit of fuss!" I shouted. "You can say that again, My life has gone bonkers and I don't understand why? I haven't seen or heard anything from you for weeks. Don't you CARE?"

Mary said nothing.

Oh! I was so upset.

Really upset. I wanted to cry.

Mary looked at me and I looked at her.

Her eyes seemed sad. Very sad.

Then,

slowly,

in the palm of her hand

a small flickering spark appeared.

It was a little… flame,

and

it burst

into

blue.

"What will be, will be?" said Mary softly. "Life tells a story."

"Does it?" I said, angrily (not understanding a thing).

Mary nodded, "yes".

then

she slowly

disappeared.

But the flame from Mary's hand remained. Hovering in the air. I think it meant something. But I didn't know what.

Then,
the flame
disappeared
and there was…

the blue butterfly.

Butterfly Blue flew around the church, and for a moment I thought everything was going to be alright. For a moment I got the feeling everything was…

…Safe.

Until…

CHAPTER 61

Anger

Suddenly, something came flying through the air. BASH. It hit me in the back. Hard

Oh, that hurt.

I turned around and looked at the ground. It was a book somebody had thrown at me. A Bible?
"There she is," a voice shouted. "The con artist."
A very old man and old woman stood watching me.
"You liar," the old woman cried. "You big filthy go-getter."
I was shocked. Their old faces looked like demons.
"Such terrible money grabbing behaviour," said the old man."
"It's an absolute DISGRACE," spat the old woman.
The old man was so angry, he suddenly held up his walking stick high in the air, and brought it down violently with a swipe. The walking stick just missed my foot.

SWIPE.
Crack.

I knew something terrible had happened. Out of so much anger, only the worst ever comes (Gran always told me that). I looked down at my feet. And... I... saw the beautiful blue butterfly lying on my shoe. I couldn't believe it. I couldn't believe what had happened.

I was heart-broken.

Oh my poor dear blue butterfly, my friend. Butterfly Blue. Gone.
Dead. Forever. Killed by an old man's walking stick. An old man,
lashing out.

Butterfly Blue
murdered
in anger.

CHAPTER 62

Grief

I could smell the old man's breath. It smelt of cabbage and peanuts. I didn't know what to say. Heartbreak is heartbreak. A tear fell down my face. But, I wasn't going to be broken by anyone. I was so hurt. But... I said nothing. The old man and woman hobbled away, muttering,
"Young people today are selfish and horrible."

When they both left the church, it was peaceful with nobody else there. Silent and still. I looked at the painting of Mary, and she looked sad. The saddest lady in the world. A little tear fell down her face in the painting, like a little star, and in the silence, I knew she understood. Mary could feel my sorrow. All the world's pain. And I knew who Mary was. A woman. A Mother (who'd lost her son. Killed). She felt my pain. And I could feel her sorrows. It was like all the world's tears were in the church for a moment. The whole world's sadness. The hurt.

I picked up
the blue butterfly
my dead friend,
and held
her blue body

in my hand.

Two broken wings.

It was a strange feeling.

Death.

And I thought, I don't feel little anymore. The world makes everybody grow up.

The blue butterfly, I buried in the rose garden in the park. One day, I knew, Butterfly Blue would grow into a beautiful blue rose.

But... I still cried... all the way home. They call it "Grief" said Gran.

"Loss."

CHAPTER 63

Trial

Mum and dad's court trial went on for weeks. They denied everything. They said me seeing Mary wasn't their idea. The vicar came to court and tried to wriggle out of everything, too. But the Judge (The Right Honourable Reginald of Pontefract) was having none of it.

"You have played a part in this money grabbing business, just like the rest of 'em."

"No, I haven't", said the vicar. "It wasn't my fault, I only charged the Queen a thousand pounds and took money off the old people for a sniff of the rose, to save my Church from being turned into luxury apartments. It was a matter of survival, Your Honour. My duty."

The Judge wasn't convinced.

"Rubbish. Is that your defence?"

The vicar said, "Yes. I never would have charged the Queen or the old people if I'd known the blue rose was a fake. I blame Holy Flo."

The judge didn't believe him. "Don't I know you? I recognise your face?" said the judge. "Good heavens! You're Reggie Stealer, the notorious con man."

"I'm not," said the vicar, frightened.

"Oh yes you are. You're not a vicar at all. You're a world class thief. The last time we met, you were pretending to be the Duchess of Scarborough!"

"Oh bother," cried the vicar, "I've been rumbled."

"Yes," said the judge. "You con people out of their money by pretending to be someone else. You're wanted by the Monte Carlo police for stealing pearls and diamond necklaces. Take him away."

"Oh, have mercy," cried the vicar (Reggie Stealer).

"No," said the judge, "You're a menace."

The vicar (Reggie Stealer) was dragged away, screaming, by four policewomen with truncheons, and locked up.

The judge next called Dad into his court. "Explain yourself," said the judge. "What is your defence?"

Dad said he wouldn't have gone to see Mr Snazzy, the agent, if I hadn't insisted on seeing Mary sat up in the branches of a tree. Mum couldn't say anything, she was on tablets. She wasn't in court. She'd been locked up in a hospital with her nerves (and that was all my fault too!). It seemed I was to blame for everything. I was the big troublemaker. Everybody said so, in the newspapers. The judge decided the only way to sort everything out, was for me to give evidence in court. He ordered me to speak.

"The truth, the whole truth, and nothing but the truth."

CHAPTER 64

Pronto

"She's under age, m'lud," said the court official.

"Holy Flo can't stand up in court and give evidence. She's too young. It's against the law."

"There's always a catch," said the judge, angrily.

The court people got together, and had a big legal conflab. They decided I could appear in court, but 'not in person.' I must give my 'evidence' from a pokey cell, underneath the courtroom with a camera pointing at my face. (This was so I wouldn't be traumatised by the Judge in his wig, shouting at me, I think.)

When I gave my evidence (my side of the story), I couldn't see the judge, and I couldn't see the jury. But they could see me in court on a big TV screen. All I could hear was the judge's voice booming down a telephone, shouting his questions. I was frightened. This Holy Flo nightmare was making me ill. I was so jittery. What the heck was happening? I'd enjoyed it at first, playing Holy Flo and flying around on a wire with a halo, but deep down, I knew it wasn't me. I was the person that liked to read, and eat sweets, and play in the park, feeding the ducks with George. I didn't want to make any of this horror happen. But then I thought, if I hadn't told people about seeing Mary, none of this would have happened. Oh, I started to get very angry again.

"Who do you think is to blame for all of this mess?" shouted the judge, down his telephone.

"I'll tell you who I think is to blame, Your Honour," I said. "It's the lady in blue. Mary is to blame for everything."

"Well," said the judge (getting more and more irritated), "we can't call her to court, can we? A sacred icon. That would be ridiculous, wouldn't it?"

"Yes," I said. "Mary only appears in public when she wants to, and that's usually sat up in the branches of a tree or hovering over the chip shop, or appearing inside the telly, or in the church or in my head."

The judge wasn't impressed with my evidence. He ordered me to see a Child Psychologist.

"Pronto."

CHAPTER 65

Daft

Dr Peabody, the famous Child Psychologist, was sent for. She arrived at court on her motor bike, with a big book of facts under her arm. She opened her book, 'Child Tantrums', and told me to look at the pictures on each page, a square, a circle, a triangle and a cat.

"Which is the odd one out?" she asked.

"The cat," I said.

"Hmmmmm," said Dr Peabody. "That's correct. What are you up to?"

"I'm up to nothing," I said.

"My tests are conclusive," said Dr Peabody. "I think this child is playing a dangerous game of cat and mouse. Florence Hargreaves is pretending she knows the correct answer to everything when really she doesn't know anything. She's a very deceptive child, indeed. One of life's pretenders. We call it in Child Psychology 'the little liar syndrome.'

What was Dr Peabody talking about?

I shouted down the telephone, "this court is daft, the grown up world is mad. You've made everything in the world complicated... but... the world is simple. All you have to do is see... the world as it really is. And that's... beautiful. And that's the truth, the whole truth, and nothing but the truth."

"Be quiet," shouted the judge, "I've heard enough lies and deceptions to last me a lifetime. Jury, give your verdict. Do you find Florence Hargreaves' mum and dad guilty or not guilty of defrauding the public and HER MAJESTY THE QUEEN of money. Did they willingly go along with their daughter's lies? Jury, make your mind up! Are they True or False? Are they…

Guilty or Not Guilty?"

CHAPTER 66

Greed

We moved back into the old house a few days later (even though it was falling down). The old house was the only place we could go to live. We had nothing left, no money. Mum and Dad were found 'guilty' by the jury, and bankrupt by the Judge. The money Mum and Dad made from me being Holy Flo had to be paid back to the old people. It was called 'compensation.' The judge said Mum and Dad should be ashamed of themselves…

"…For being such greedy hoodwinkers and letting your greed run wild. You should have told your awful daughter to stop playing games and making stories up, instead of encouraging her to make money out of her pathetic desires for attention. There's too many young people wanting to be rich and famous nowadays, and it's got to stop. If we carry on like this, who will be left to sweep the streets and empty the dustbins? Everybody will be living in Hollywood, believing they're a star."

Mum and Dad were ordered to polish old people's shoes for five years.
"This is a heavy sentence," said the Judge, "a warning to others, that giving is much better than stealing."
Mum and Dad wouldn't speak to me. They blamed me for ruining their lives. They sent me to bed with no dinner for six weeks. I wasn't allowed out. Gran tried to cheer me up. She said it wasn't me who was to blame. Gran said, "things just got out of control,

like a snowball rolling faster and faster down a mountain, and growing bigger and bigger until it was a full scale avalanche."

But, I wouldn't listen to Gran. I was furious and angry, not with Gran but with someone else.

"Why didn't Mary stop it?" I said. "Why did she let this happen?"

"I don't know," said Gran. "It's a… mystery."

CHAPTER 67

Lost

I didn't want to see Mary anymore. She'd kept very quiet throughout the court case. The more I thought about Mary the more furious I got.

Then, one night, just when I was falling asleep,

she appeared again,
hovering
in my bedroom.

Mary didn't say anything. She just floated inside a moonbeam, like a moth. There was no saying "sorry" to me. Nothing. So, I just pulled the duvet over my head, and shouted, "Go away! I don't want to see you. I thought you were my friend. You said you were my friend. But you're not my friend. You're just like everyone else."

"I am your friend," said Mary, softly.

"No, you're not, you're just the same as George. I thought he was my friend and he wasn't."

"Sometimes," said Mary, "friends don't always behave like you want them to."

"You can say that again."

"Sometimes," said Mary, "life doesn't always go the way you think it should."

"You can say that again."

"Sometimes, things happen for a reason, but at the time the reason isn't clear."

"What are you talking about, Mary?" I said.

"All will be revealed."

I was fed up of Mary talking in riddles, I threw my pillow at her. "Go away," I shouted. "I've had enough of you and your make-believe. I want my life to feel normal again. Ordinary."

Mary said nothing.
She smiled,
softly,
sadly,
tenderly.

Then she faded
away,
into
the moon's beam.

"Good riddance," I cried. "I never want to talk to you again."

And from that night, I didn't. I didn't talk with Mary at all. If I'm being honest, I secretly waited for her to come back. But nothing. No Mary. She'd left me for good.
Gone.
Forever.
and I cried
and
I cried.

I felt alone. More alone than ever. And I felt…

…lost.

CHAPTER 68

Chips

Mum went back to work on the till at the supermarket, and Dad went back cleaning windows up his ladder. They both went cleaning old people's shoes in the evenings and always came back stinking of polish. Mum and Dad were bad tempered and exhausted all the time. I was left on my own. We couldn't find a school that would have me. They all said I was 'a hot potato they wouldn't handle.' I had so much time on my hands, I didn't know what to do. One afternoon I sneaked out of the house. I decided I'd walk to the chip shop and buy myself some chips, like I used to with George. I was trying to make everything seem normal again, like once upon a time.

When I walked into the chip shop, guess what? Who should I see standing in the queue... but... him, George. I wondered whether he'd say "hello", but no, after he bought his chips, he just lowered his eyes and walked away. I thought, walk away, then. See if I care. But I did care. I cared a lot. Seeing George made me think how much my life had changed since we were friends. Life was easier back then. It was just about being friendly and liking people. I bought my chips, and started to walk home, wondering if I'd ever feel happy again? But after a minute or two I felt like someone was watching. I thought it might be Mary. I turned around and I saw... George. He was following me.

"What do you want?" I shouted.

George didn't answer. He ran away. I walked quickly back along the street and followed him around the corner. George was standing there, blowing on a chip, pretending he couldn't see me. It was a strange moment, like we were both invisible. Like we didn't know each other. But we did know each other.

"Why didn't you stand up for me?" I said. "And tell everyone we saw Mary?"

George didn't answer. He didn't say a word. Then, he suddenly shouted,

"Ahhhhhhhhhhh."

He threw his chips on the ground like he was crazy. "What's the matter with you?" I said, shocked. George turned to look at me. And I looked at him. We stood like this for a long time. It seemed forever. Neither of us giving in. My heart was beating. Fast. My breathing was going in and out, in and out. I felt anxious, worried, stressed. I thought I might fall over. I was angry and worried, anxious and stressed, all at the same time. And I could tell George felt the same. He was trembling.

CHAPTER 69

Imagination

His eyes were red. George seemed really, really sad, but trying to hide it. I closed my eyes. I didn't want him to see I was upset too (almost crying). I was too proud.

"What's that yellow stain doing on your back?" said George, softly. I didn't answer (it was too upsetting). Then I thought, no, I will say, because you're partly to blame for it.

"A woman chucked an egg at me…" I said. "…this morning. She thought I needed taking down a peg or two."

"Why?" said George.

"You know why. People hate me. The whole flipping world hates me, because of the lady in blue."

"Oh," said George.

He didn't know what to do. He was embarrassed. Then, he said, softly,

"Well… I don't hate you."

George looked me in the eyes. His eyes were beautiful. Blue.

"I wish I was like you." He said. "You see things most people can't see. I wish I was born with an imagination. You'll be an artist one day, or a poet, or a writer. I know it."

"If you think that," I said, "why did you drop me as a friend?"

George shrugged. A tear fell down his face (guilty or what?).

"Sometimes, "said George, "you can't always do the things you should do."

"You're talking daft, George, like Mary."

"Nobody's perfect, are they?"

"Nobody's perfect?" I said. "You can say that again."

George took out his handkerchief and blew his nose. He looked different. He looked sort of taller. And then I thought, I know what's different. George looks older. More grown up.

"Tomorrow," said George, "I want you to do something. Will you?"

"What?"

"Tomorrow, at 5 o'clock, switch on your telly."

"Why?"

"You'll see, Flo. I promise. All will be revealed." And George walked away.

CHAPTER 70

Tell

Oh my goodness!!! I couldn't believe it. I switched on the telly the next day… and… there was George being interviewed on the Gloria Riccardo show! I couldn't believe what I was seeing.

What was George up to?

"Tell my viewers everything," said Gloria. "The full story of your friendship with Florence Hargreaves. We want to know the truth, the whole truth, and nothing but the truth. Did she try and make you say you'd seen Mother Mary sat up in a tree? Did she want you to partake in her lies?"

I thought, what are you trying to do, George, appearing on TV, and talking about me like this? I'm trying to forget about it all.

"She's a disgrace," burped George's Dad (sat next to George).
The TV audience started shouting, "FOR SHAME. FOR SHAME."
Gloria quickly waved her microphone to keep the TV audience quiet.
"Silence," she shouted. "Let this innocent boy speak. This is a very serious moment in broadcasting history. Go on, George, tell us your side of the story. This boy is here today to reveal the truth."

The TV audience started to lean forward, listening hard. Everybody wanted to hear what George had to say about me. George seemed pale, nervous. He took a deep breath and started to speak (looking into the TV camera).

"Yes. It's time I told you everything," said George. "I wish… I'd told you from the start, because it might… have saved… a lot of trouble."

"Why?" asked Gloria. She seemed slightly confused. "What are you saying?"

"The truth," said George. "Me and Flo… did see the lady in blue sat up in the branches of a tree."

"Pardon?" said Gloria, gobsmacked.

"Eh?" shouted George's dad, spilling his lager.

"Flo Hargreaves is not a liar," George said. "She's a very special person. She sees things in the everyday, when playing, that most people will never be able to see in a lifetime, and when you're with her, sometimes you can see things too. That's what Flo's like. She's full of wonder."

"Oh, George!"

My heart was thumping.
George was making
my heart
skip and jump
(in a good way).

Gloria's TV show wasn't going to plan. It was obvious she'd hoped George was going to come on TV and dish some dirt. But he hadn't.

"Explain yourself," said Gloria. "Are you saying Florence Hargreaves speaks the truth? She sees… things?"

"Yes," said George.

"Magical things."

"Mysterious things."

"Mystical things."

"Take no notice," said George's dad, "the boy's crazy. His poor mother will be turning in her grave."

"No she won't," said George angrily. "Mum won't be turning in her grave from what I'm saying. She'll be turning in her grave because of you."

I thought his dad might explode. His face went purple. He couldn't stand what George was saying.

"Shut it," said George's dad.

But George wouldn't stop. "After Mum died, I tried to make you happy, Dad. I stopped seeing Flo when you said you were lonely, but it made no difference. You just ignored me. You didn't know I was there most of the time, because of your drinking."

George's dad tried to stand up. He wobbled.

"You care more about that girl than me!" he cried.

"No I don't," said George. "I care about you both, but I'm not going to kill my friendship with Flo anymore, just because you're jealous. You're frightened of facing the world, Dad. You're lonely since Mum died. You're a drunk!"

"Oh! How very true," said Gloria. "Let me put your father in touch with a bereavement counsellor. Let me heal your father's pain."

George's dad did look sad. His bottom lip started to quiver. It was very upsetting. He made big gulping noises, like a fish. His tears were like water spurting out of a shower. I'd never seen a grown up man cry. A Dad! George's eyes were filling up, too. One or two tears began to trickle down his face like little rain drops. Oh dear. It was very very sad, very upsetting to see.

"Don't cry, Dad, please," whispered George. "Please."

"You see, this is what happens, ladies and gentlemen," said Gloria, "when two people become lost. Only my help can rebuild a father and son's life back together again."

"Shut up," cried George.

"What?" Gloria looked amazed.

George went more red and purple than his dad. He shook like a boiling kettle. He jumped up from his chair and ran at Gloria. It was like he was going to… punch her!

"I said, SHUT YOUR BIG MOUTH!"

"Security!" screamed Gloria, in shock.

The TV audience started shouting and whooping. They were really enjoying the show.

"You see what Flo Hargreaves has done!?" cried Gloria.

"She's caused a middle aged father to become a drunk and a young son to become a violent juvenile delinquent."

"Flo hasn't done anything of the sort," shouted George.

"Oooooooooooooooh!" cried the TV audience.

"Flo Hargreaves is a good person."

"Flo Hargreaves is a liar" shouted Gloria.

"No she's not. You're the liar," shouted George.

150

George looked into the TV camera and started talking to me, at home.

"Gloria Riccardo is a big phoney, isn't she, Flo? She's nothing like she seems on TV. She smokes like a chimney, drinks bottles of whisky, eats meat pies, and her breath stinks."

"How dare you!?" screamed Gloria.

But George hadn't finished sticking the boot in. Not yet. There was more.

"Listen to me, everyone," cried George. "Wait until I tell you… this!"

George grabbed the TV microphone off Gloria. It was George's big TV moment.

"Gloria Riccardo claims she's a caring person and wants to help people," he cried, "but all she cares about is her TV show. She hates people. She only makes this programme to make herself look special, but she isn't special, or good. She's horrible."

"Ohhhhhhhhhhhhhhhhhhhhhh!" cried the TV audience.

Gloria glared at George. You could tell she wanted to punch him in the face. Hard. Then suddenly, someone in the audience shouted, "Hear hear!"

Guess what?

It was Gran sat in the front row of the audience. "I believe everything that boy is saying," shouted Gran.

Oh, I couldn't believe it!

Then, someone else shouted, "Hear hear! I believe it too, there's something nasty and smelly lurking under Gloria's hair-do."

Guess what?

It was the butcher (the one that gave Gran a pound of free sausages). They must have been on a secret date. They were both holding hands!

"How dare you speak to me like this?" hissed Gloria. "I'm a STAR."

"Boooooooo." shouted the TV audience.

The audience didn't give a monkey's about Gloria anymore. They believed Gran! They agreed with the butcher! They agreed with George!

"She's a phoney!" shouted George. "Gloria Riccardo is a two-faced COW! "

Suddenly, Vera, the make-up man appeared from behind a camera.

"Yes," he shouted "I agree with every single word."

Gloria looked very scared. "Listen to me, viewers," cried Vera. "I've done Riccardo's hair and make-up for twenty five years. And in all that time, she's never once said thank you or bought me a box of chocolates. And if it wasn't for me, Gloria Riccardo wouldn't look like a glamorous TV Star. Oh no! She'd look like.................... this!"

Vera pulled off Gloria's wig.

Oh, Vera!

He threw the wig into the audience. The audience started to grab at the wig like tigers killing a furry rabbit in a jungle. Gloria stood staring in shock. Her real hair was wispy and grey. Nearly bald! She looked about 92! Gloria went mental. She jumped on Vera like a panther and tried to scratch his eyes out, but Vera was too quick for her. He pushed Gloria over. She fell. The TV audience roared, "Fight! Fight! Fight!" Gloria and Vera started rolling and rolling around the floor. It was a wrestling match.

"Bitch!" screamed Vera.
"Queen! "screamed Gloria.
"Bitch!"
"Queen!"

The T.V audience shouted "Fight Fight Fight"

It was car crash TV, the audience screaming with laughter. Gloria and Vera rolling and fighting, both covered in dirt and dust, It was………….. Unbelievable. George quickly got out of their way. He looked into the TV camera.

Then, George held his thumb up and winked, and I knew who that wink and thumbs up was for.

It was for me!
George and me were friends again.
Hurrah!
Hurrah!
Hurrah!

CHAPTER 71

Miracle

"You're my hero," I said.

"Don't talk daft," said George, blushing.

Me and George were sat on a bench in the park, beside the duck pond.

"I'm sorry for not saying anything sooner, Flo."

"You did it when you could, George."

"Yes, I suppose. But if I'd been brave and stood up for you in the beginning, none of this business of you being called a world class liar would have happened."

"They'd have just called us both liars, George."

"Perhaps."

Me and George walked over to the pond and threw some bread to the ducks. The ducks were pleased. It was an autumn day. I looked around the park and I saw Mary's tree. It was losing its leaves. The tree would soon be falling asleep for the winter.

"Do you really believe miracles happen?" I said.

"Yes, of course, Flo. Miracles happen every day."

"How do we know, George?"

"Well… that tree is a miracle.

That duck is a miracle.

I'm a miracle.

You're a miracle.

Knowing each other in the world, being friends,

…is a miracle."

I was pleased George said this. I was glad he could still see the world like we'd always seen it, when playing.

"I'd rather see the world through your eyes, Flo, any day, than the way most people see it."

That's what George said. Beautiful, don't you think?

After feeding the ducks, me and George decided to walk through the park together, like old times.
"How's your dad?" I asked
"Fine," said George. "He's going to AA."
"What's that?"
"Well, it's not my Aunty Annie's. It's a place where drunks go to start feeling better. It stands for Alcoholics Anonymous."
"Will it take him a long time to get better?"
"Who knows? But he's not been drinking since he went, so that makes things a lot easier at home. There's some hope."
"Good," I said.
Me and George walked through the park for some time. Everything was changing. You could feel it in the air, a crispness. Soon the flowers would all disappear, and not come back until the spring.
"How's your mum and dad doing?" asked George.
"They keep blaming each other for everything," I said. "They've decided to get a divorce."
"How do you feel about that?"
"Well, I'm not pleased, but I'm going to live with my gran while they sort themselves out, so living with Gran will be OK, won't it?"

"Yes, she's a nice woman, your gran. I like her."

"Me too."

We stopped walking and I was thinking how good it was to be George's friend again.

"Seeing Mary, up in the branches of a tree," I said, "brought about a lot of mischief, didn't it?"

"That's true," laughed George.

George looked at me and I looked at him. He smiled. And I smiled back. It felt lovely.

We turned up another path and walked some more. We stopped to breathe the clean, fresh air...

and

then

suddenly…

there

she was.

Like the first day
we saw her.

Mary, sat up in the branches of a tree.

CHAPTER 72

Story

"Hello, dears," said Mary. "Life is very complicated at times, don't you think?"

"Yes," I said.

"Yes," said George.

"The world is a very difficult place, sometimes," sighed Mary, softly.

"Then why do you come here?" I asked.

"Well… everybody has their part to play, don't they? "said Mary.

I didn't say anything. I'd just finished playing my part as 'Holy Flo' and look what trouble that had caused.

"What's my part in all of this?" asked George.

"You?" said Mary. "Your part, at present, is talking to me and Florence."

"Why?"

"It's part of the story."

"What story?" I asked.

"Our story," said Mary. "The story we make happen each day."

"I don't understand," said George.

"All will be revealed," said Mary.

"You keep on saying that," I said.

"Well, that's because it will be," said Mary.

"Everything is revealed in the end."

In the palm of Mary's hand
a small flickering spark appeared.

It was a little… flame (again),
and
it burst
into

blue.

"What's that?" asked George, amazed.
The light was so bright it almost hurt our eyes.
"It's a spark." Mary said. "The spark in everything… the spark of
life."

Suddenly the spark grew brighter and brighter. Like a star
(blinding).

Then… FLASH
Mary held the rose.

"It's the blue rose," I gasped.
"Yes," said Mary.

The three of us looked at the rose.
For a moment, all was quiet.
Even
the birds were
silent.

CHAPTER 73

Heart

The world was still. Only the faint thumping of three hearts. Me, George, and Mary.

I needed to ask Mary one or two more things. The things I still didn't understand.

I said, "if the blue rose was sucked up the nozzle of a hoover, and it was replaced, how come the old people started to dance when they sniffed it?"

"They danced because they believed in the rose," said Mary. "And they fell down once they didn't believe in the rose anymore. We all have to believe in something, don't we?"

"Yes," I said.

Mary held the blue rose up into the air. We could smell the rose's perfume, floating everywhere. It was like...

summer,
autumn,
winter,
spring.

All the days

mixed up
together,
with a hint of the sun,
and the moon and the stars.

Heavenly.

We closed our eyes and inhaled everything, and for a moment, it felt like everything in the world was the same. Me, George, and Mary. The trees, the flowers, the grass, the sun, didn't feel like separate things. It all felt... like... one.

one thing,
one world,
beautiful.

Then, we opened our eyes and George said,
"What happens now?"
"What do you mean?" asked Mary.
"Will people believe us, if we say we've seen you again?"
"Probably not," said Mary. "But a few people might."

Mary looked across the park towards the church. A 'For Sale' sign was being nailed to a wall by a man.
"People forget about things very quickly, don't they?" sighed Mary.

She seemed sad for a moment. Like she was thinking deeply. Then, Mary floated down from the tree, and started to walk along a path which led to the rose garden. She held the blue rose next to her heart.

We followed.

CHAPTER 74

Eternal

"Where are you going?" asked George.

"I'm going to see my son," said Mary. "He's waiting for me in the rose garden."

"But I thought…"

"Yes?" said Mary.

"I thought your son was dead," I said, nervously. "I thought Jesus was killed?"

Mary stopped walking.

"He was," said Mary. She looked at me. Mary said nothing. She looked into my eyes deeply for some time, then said, "Things like that happen sometimes, don't they? When there isn't enough… love in the world."

"I suppose," I said (I still didn't really understand).

I wanted to ask more, like, how can you talk to someone if they're dead, but I didn't.

"It's all written down in the story," Mary said. "The story that never ends. Nothing ever dies." Mary opened the gate to the rose garden. "Everything lives on and on in some way. Forever."

The Eternal.

"Will we see you again?" asked George.

"Yes," said Mary "I never go away."

Mary smiled.

"I'm here always."

A leaf floated gently down from a tree.

I picked up the leaf and put it in my pocket.

I wanted to keep the leaf to remind me of today.

The day I could see and hear special things.

The day I... believed.

CHAPTER 75

Beautiful

"What are you two doing?" called Gran, walking towards us. She was carrying two bags of shopping.

"We're talking to Mary again," I said.

"Oh, is she well?" asked Gran

"Yes," I said.

"Good." said Gran, smiling. "I'm glad to hear it. Where is she?"

I looked at George. He looked at me. We both looked around for Mary.

"She's just… gone," George said.

"Oh what a pity," said Gran "I'd like to have met her. Just the once. Never mind."

The three of us started walking along the path together.

"Are you both busy?" asked Gran. "Because I've just bought a large bag of potatoes. How do you both fancy coming back to my laundrette, and I'll make us some chips?"

"Great," said George.

"Will you fry them in the old fashioned way?" I said.

"Of course," said Gran, "I'll fry them the chip shop way. What other way is there?"

We went back with Gran and had some chips and they were delicious.

After that day we both never saw Mary again, when playing.

Me and George started to do other things, like swimming and going to see a film, and hanging around shopping malls. People did stop and ask us about Mary for a bit. But in the end the newspapers and telly people lost interest. They started telling other people's stories. Footballers, pop stars, movie stars and the like.

From time to time, Gran and me walked over to the church (before they turned it into luxury apartments) and I'd light a candle beside Mary's painting. And sometimes, if you looked very carefully at the painting, it seemed like Mary knew we were there, and it seemed like she was listening.

"I'm glad you came to visit us, Mary. I really am. Thank you for letting me be part of the story."

And it seemed like Mary understood, because she always seemed to smile back. And once, she might have even winked.
Mysteriously.
And when she did this, I always felt something deep, deep, deep in my heart.
And the best word to describe it,
this feeling, is… gladness. I was glad.

CHAPTER 76

Dream

The night before my 16th birthday,
something strange
happened.

A dream,
and my dream
went like this…

I was lying in bed, then all of a sudden, I was floating out of the window, I was floating over fields of flowers. The flowers were different colours, they were glowing like a thousand electric lightbulbs. Ever so bright and colourful, like the coloured lights on a Christmas tree. They smelt of my favourite sweets, and I thought to myself, what a way to travel! It beats riding on a bus.

And when I thought of a bus ride, I thought of her, sat next to me, like the day she gave me the gift of the blue rose. And when I thought of her, there she was, lying next to me.

Both floating over the fields of electric lightbulb flowers.

Together.
Holding hands.

And when I looked down, one of the flowers sparkled more than
the others. Its light was so bright. I knew the light meant
something, but I wasn't sure what. Until suddenly the light shone
even brighter, a flame,
and
it burst
into

blue.

And then, I felt Mary squeeze my hand tenderly.
And her hand felt as real as George's hand.
And my dream made me feel everything was true.
Anything in life can happen.
Anything in life is possible.

When you believe.

When you see.

When you know…

the moon is…

blue.

CHAPTER 77

Love

It was summer in the park. George, 16 years old, was lying next to me. His eyes were closed, sleeping. We were holding hands. George slowly awoke. He looked at me. He smiled. We both looked up into the branches of the tree.
George said, "What can you see? Can you see anything, Flo?"
And I said, "Oh yes, I can see something."
"What can you see?" said George.

"I can see everything," I said. "I can see every possibility."

And I was smiling. And George smiled back.

And then, George put his arms around me and held me close,
and me and George
kissed.

And I felt…

Love.

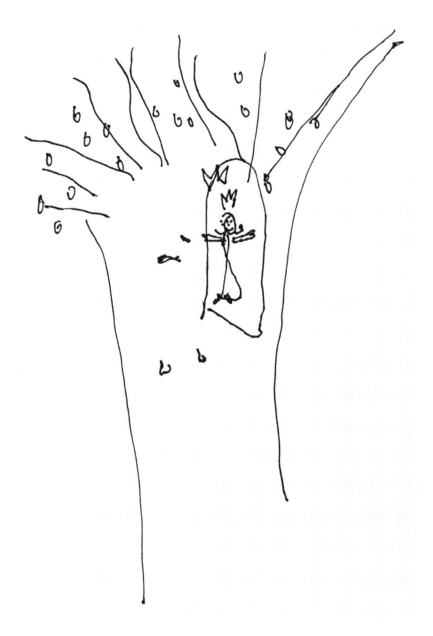

'The lady up in a tree' by Martyn Hesford

Printed in Great Britain
by Amazon

70624190R00102